JANIE'S GOT A GUN

Crime Fiction Inspired by the Music
of Aerosmith

Edited by
Michael Bracken

White City

Press

Other Music Themed Anthologies from White City Press

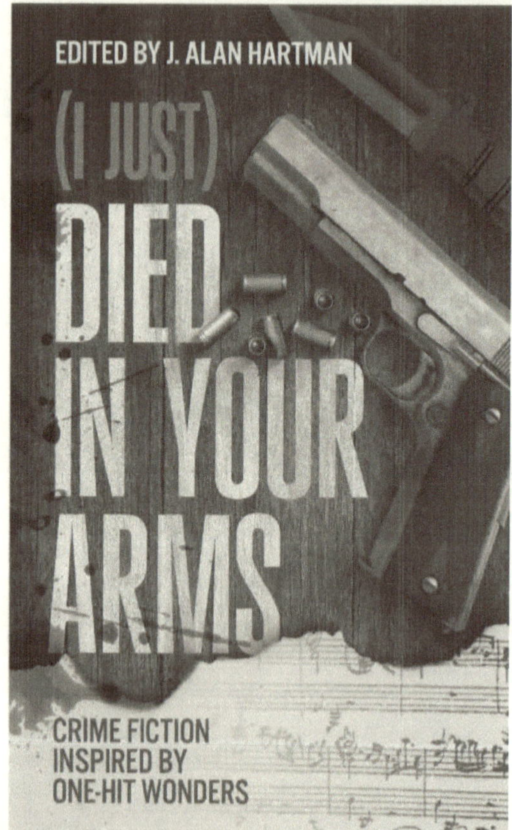

Hitting the charts only once isn't just unfortunate...it's a crime.

Over the decades, tons of musical artists and groups have had a hit song that has lived on long after the tune topped the charts and is often looked upon fondly for decades to come. For some musicians, this may be the only the song they're ever known for and they fade into obscurity soon thereafter. These are affectionately known as "one-hit wonders," and are much celebrated by fans and music publications, particularly on September 25th each year on One-Hit Wonder Day

12 of today's best short story authors have taken their favorite one-hit wonders and reimagined them as the influence for some pretty heinous crimes. *(I Just) Died in Your Arms* features a decades-spanning collection of immediately recognizable hit songs turned into stories from the amazing talents of Vinnie Hansen, Jeanne DuBois, Josh Pachter, J.M. Taylor, Christine Verstraete, Sandra Murphy, Joseph S. Walker, Wendy Harrison, Bev Vincent, Leone Ciporin, Adam Gorgoni and Barb Goffman.

Paperback ISBN: 9781963479027 eBook ISBN 9781963479010

JANIE'S GOT A GUN

Crime Fiction Inspired by the Music of Aerosmith

Edited by
Michael Bracken

Published by White City Press
An imprint of Misti Media LLC
https://whitecitypress.com
Available in both Paperback and eBook Editions
1 2 3 4 5 6 7 8 9 10
Copyright © Respective Authors 2024
Paperback ISBN: 9781963479539
eBook ISBN: 9781963479522

Dedication

For Temple
My Love, My Muse, My Everything

CONTENTS

Dream On

(From the album, Aerosmith)

Ed Ridgley

"I knew a man who was so lazy it was lucky breathing was automatic." David Douglas always opened his self-help seminars with this anecdote.

He loosened his tie when he saw his high school bully, Max Munson, off to the right. It was the tenth time he had seen him at his seminars.

"Now…uh…now…uh. Excuse me," he said and coughed.

"Now while you may laugh at that, and I hope you did, I want to tell you that that man"—he paused for effect—"was me."

Max was gone and David let out a sigh. Taking in a deep breath, he continued.

"See, I was so lazy that I could not get myself out of bed to face the day. I had no drive. I had no vision. I had no anything. I was fresh out of college, working a nine-to-five job, and going nowhere in the fast lane and feeling as empty as a poor man's pockets."

"What changed, you may ask. Well, I'll tell you."

David saw Max now to his left and felt his face flush with anger.

Louder with each word, he said, "My Frontier changed. And it can change for you as well. Your Frontier is not a fad or a phase or a phony phrase. Say that three times real fast."

David's helpers led the laughter for the audience.

"It's a way of life. And it can change your life."

Seeing no sign of the bully, he sighed again.

"Now you may be thinking, David, this sounds like another self-help program, and I say to that, this is a self-awakening program. To which you might say, David, you're putting lipstick on a pig. Well, we can debate all day long till the cows…you know the saying. But where does that get us? I'll tell you where it gets us."

He gritted his teeth when he saw Max near the stage, composed himself, broke into a grin, and began speaking louder and louder.

"It gets us going a hundred miles an hour toward a dead-end road in a dead-end town on a dead-end day is where it gets us." He looked over to his right but didn't see Max, and he let out a long sigh.

"You are here today for a purpose, and I'm guessing it's not to get into an argument so much as to get into an agreement, an agreement with yourself. From cradle to grave, what are you going to do in between? From bassinette to burial, what is your decision today? Will you find Your Frontier? Well, will you?"

The helpers started the applause that set the emotional mood on fire. He clapped with them until he saw Max again. David walked over to his assistant.

"Take over for me for a minute. I need to take a quick break," he said.

"Sure thing, boss."

* * *

"I've heard some hogwash but that was an extra helping of it," Max said.

"What are you doing here?" David asked. "How did you get backstage?"

"There's never enough security, is there?"

"What are you doing here?"

"I had to see how little Davey was doing. You've done pretty good for yourself, haven't you?"

"I work hard."

"Yeah, whatever. You got lucky."

"I didn't get lucky. I've worked long and hard for what I have. What have you done?"

"Don't worry about me. What would all these people say if they knew how little Davey would run scared every time somebody walked up to him?"

"What is your point?"

"Davey—"

"I'm not Davey. I'm David."

"Davey, you live on a stack of shit. Why does luck get to pick you and not me?"

"How am I to blame for that?"

Max moved within inches of David, looked down at him, and whispered, "Don't make me finish what I started years ago."

"You don't scare me anymore."

Max pushed him backward. David lost his footing and fell.

"I can have you arrested."

"My word against yours," Max said.

* * *

Hearing those words reminded David of the time in high school when Max would torment him. "My word against yours," he would always say when David said he would report him.

"You need to stand up to him," David's stepbrother told him.

"He's way bigger than me."

"Kick him in the groin and then hit him in the nose. And keep kicking him till he quits saying stop."

"Don't you mean till he starts saying stop?"

"If he can talk, he can get up. You must teach these guys a lesson, Davey. And the only lesson they understand is a good ass whipping."

"I'm not a kicking and hitting kind of guy."

"Well, then, you better start loving pain. It's either his pain or your pain."

* * *

The next day at school David had to recite "Ozymandias" in front of the class with a black eye, a fat lip, and a loose tooth.

"Half sunk a shattered visage lies, whose frown, and wrinkled lip…"

He stopped and rubbed his lower lip.

"Come on, Davey. We don't have all day," Max said.

"Quiet, class," the teacher said. "Go on, Davey."

He continued with the remaining four lines.

"Look on my Works, ye Mighty, and despair! Nothing beside remains. Round the decay of that colossal Wreck, boundless and bare the lone and level sands stretch far away."

"Very good, Davey," the teacher said.

"And that's what happens to bullies," David said.

"Yes, that's right, Davey. The poet, Percy Bysshe Shelley, was bullied and probably had that in mind when he wrote the poem."

* * *

At a book signing for his self-help book *Your Frontier*, David told the crowd, "The idea for my philosophy came to me one day when I had to recite the poem 'Ozymandias.' It's a great poem. If you haven't read it, you should. It's my favorite. It ends with, 'the lone and level sands stretch far away.' From that line, from those words, on that day, the idea for *Your Frontier* was born. I had been bullied during that time. That poem showed me, promised me, that the bully's time came to an end at the beginning of my frontier, that my frontier had no boundaries and no limits. I could be anything I wanted to be. I could do anything I wanted to do. And you can too."

* * *

"We're not in high school anymore," David said. "Why do you keep harassing me?"

"I think you are completely full of shit is why. You're making all kinds of stupid money from some stupid sayings," Max said.

"You should maybe read my book."

"Yeah, right."

"So how does this end? Are you going to just keep showing up everywhere I go?"

"I haven't decided yet."

"I don't have time for this," David said, and he turned to go back on stage.

Max grabbed his shoulder and spun him around. David clenched his fists and his face turned red.

"Oh, little Davey is getting mad."

David shook his head, unclenched his fists, and rubbed his face.

"You know what, come on stage with me."

"Yeah, that ain't gonna happen."

"I didn't think you were a coward."

"Don't call me a coward."

David returned to the stage.

* * *

"Ladies and gentlemen, thank you for your patience. Thank you, Calvin, for standing in my stead. A round of applause, everybody, for my assistant, Calvin."

The helpers led the applause.

"Ladies and gentlemen, I often give cursory examples of *Your Frontier*, but tonight I want to give you a hands-on demonstration. You're in for a treat, both for you and for me. I've never done this, so we'll see how this plays out. What do you say?"

The helpers led the applause again.

"There is someone in the audience tonight who is none other than my high school bully, Max Munson. Max, come on up here, would you?"

"Get bent," Max yelled.

"Come on, Max," David urged.

Max gave him the finger.

"Ladies and gentlemen, I think Max has some stage fright. Let's help him out, shall we?"

The helpers led the applause.

"Do it, Max," an audience member said.

"Get on up there," another said.

"Don't chicken out, Max," said another.

"Yeah, don't be a coward, Max," one of the helpers shouted.

"Don't call me a coward," Max yelled.

Max gave the finger to the audience, climbed the steps to the stage, and glared at David.

"Max, how can I help you?"

"Help me? I don't need no help."

"Everybody needs help of some kind. I did when we were kids."

"Yeah, you sicked your stepbrother on me, but he ain't here to help you now, is he?"

"No, he isn't. I don't need him anymore."

"You probably have security guards now."

"I waved them off. It's just me and you talking now. No need for violence."

"That was your first mistake."

David had heard those words before back in high school when Max confronted him about his stepbrother's threats. He tried to shake his head of the memory.

"Hey," Max said, now on stage.

David shook his head again remembering the rest of the scene from long ago.

"You need to meet my five friends, the knuckle family," Max had said back then.

David shook his head a third time and tried to compose himself.

"I said I don't need no help," Max said, and shoved David, causing him to lose his balance and fall. He scrambled back to his feet. His clenched fists caused his knuckles to turn as white as chalk. His face was as red as a raging fire. He shook his head and thought, "I don't want to do this. Not here. Not now of all places. I don't want to do this."

David turned and lurched toward Max and connected with a quick left and then a quick right.

He remembered what his stepbrother had told him. "Kick him in the groin and then hit him in the nose. And keep kicking him till he quits saying stop.

David smashed Max's nose with his palm. He kicked him in the groin. He planted a fist in his stomach. And then a left to the jaw. And a right and a left. And another right and a left. Max yelled "stop" but David kept punching him.

Max started sobbing.

David shook his head. "Oh," he said and shook his head again. He looked at Max and then he looked at the crowd. The women had their hands over their mouths. The men looked stunned, with their jaws dropped.

David straightened his shirt and tie and smiled.

"Well, I guess I made my point, didn't I?"

The helpers started to laugh, causing the audience to join them. The security guards took Max offstage as David continued.

"It's either their pain or your pain."

This time, the audience erupted in applause without the helpers' encouragement.

* * *

David Douglas launched his second book tour and seminar with *Testing Your Frontier* to a large group of attendees.

"My first book *Your Frontier* brought you to the edge of your existence. Now with *Testing Your Frontier*, you can go further. Further than you ever thought possible—or could ever imagine."

Same Old Song and Dance
(From the album, Get Your Wings)
Bill Baber

My old man always said that if you were a Mick born on the southside, you came out of the womb with two strikes against you. He also said the only hope for an Irishman from this part of town was to go into politics or the mob—he chose the latter. After years of fouling off pitches, his third strike came from a load of double-aught buckshot courtesy of Danny Riordan.

As a result of his murder, I chose politics. But the harsh reality was that politics and the mob on the southside were joined at the hip. And both were equally deadly.

For twenty years Kevin Flynn had run the Fifth Ward. And he was as crooked as that street in San Francisco. The unions kept him in power—as did the Irish mob. But the neighborhood was changing, becoming gentrified. Young professionals were taking advantage of cheaper housing prices, and the Irish were no longer a majority on the southside.

A heavy rain was falling the morning Flynn called me to his office. It had rained the day my father was murdered. After that, I always thought rain fell like tears on the southside, and no amount could cleanse the sins and blood that stained the streets.

Flynn was not a tall man, but he seemed large. He had thick, curly gray hair, icy blue eyes, and a nose that had been broken a time or two. His cheeks were ruddy, and his appearance gave the impression that Kevin Flynn was someone you did not fool with. For some reason, however, he did not scare me.

I had headed the city's planning commission for several years and had butted heads with Flynn on several occasions when he sought favors to get projects approved that would line his pockets. I held no animosity toward him—at least not then—and considered all proposals that came before the commission on their merits and if they would benefit or detract from the vision the city had set forth for its future.

Flynn's office was fancy, a large mahogany desk flanked by two carved wooden chairs with maroon cushions that matched the drapes framing an oversized window facing the desk. There were paintings of The Emerald Isle with ornate, gilded frames and a bookshelf with first editions of famed Irish poets and authors. A separate table held a crystal decanter and matching glasses.

He sat behind the desk, intensely studying some documents when I entered. He ignored me for a minute or two. Then, without looking up, he finally acknowledged me.

"Patrick Flaherty, always good to see you, lad," he said with an effected brogue. He grew up three blocks from where I did. He rose from the desk and offered his hand. His grip was strong, and he looked me directly in the eye as we shook hands.

"Get you a drink?" he said.

"Thanks, but no. It's a little early for me."

"Nonsense. It's never too early for a taste of Ireland's finest."

He poured two stiff shots, handing one to me and gesturing me to a chair.

He lifted his glass. "To your health."

After he drank, he asked, "How is your mother fairing?"

"She's fine. Look Mr. Flynn, let's cut to the chase. You didn't summon me here to talk about my mother."

"That is true, Patrick. I know this city is changing and some are anxious to change the way things have always been done on the southside. Those changes may come someday but now is not the time."

He got up and poured himself another taste. I hadn't touched mine.

"There is a project that will be coming before the planning commission. I—and the neighborhood—need your vote. It will create good paying jobs while it is being built and after as well."

"I'm familiar with the project. To be perfectly honest, it's a strip mall that doesn't align with the city's General Plan."

I could see the anger flare in Flynn's cheeks. He reached into a desk drawer and pulled out a thick envelope.

"Ten thousand for your vote Patrick. And if you work with us, there's plenty more where that came from."

He got up to pour another drink. I stood as well.

"I'm not for sale. This is exactly what we're trying to change. It's the same old song and dance, the same old story. It's time for it to end."

He gritted his teeth.

"You're a stubborn son of a bitch—just like your old man. And look what that got him."

I threw a right hand that started from the tips of my toes. Blood splattered as the punch added to the tally of broken noses Flynn had suffered. The force of the blow sent him sprawling across the desk. With a look of hatred in his eyes, he said, "You will pay a heavy price for that."

* * *

Later that day I met Mike Quinn at a bar downtown. We had been best friends since sixth grade, played basketball together at Saint Aloysius High School and roomed together in college. He went on to earn a law degree and was an up-and-coming defense attorney. I told him what happened with Flynn.

"You got a pair on ya, that's for sure. I can't believe you decked Kevin Flynn. Rumor is the last guy did that ended up in a barrel out in the bay."

"I think he had something to do with my old man's death," I said.

I had never known the circumstances surrounding my father's murder. The rumor was Riordan killed him over a gambling debt he owed Lefty Shannon. It added up because the old man was a gambling degenerate. Ponies, football, boxing, you name it, seemed he always had a bet down but rarely won.

"How are you going to find out anything about it now?" Quinn asked.

"I'm going to talk to Riordan. See what he has to say."

Quinn looked at me like I had lost my mind.

"You got a death wish today? First, you clock Flynn, now you want to talk to one of the most dangerous men in the state. What do you think he might do if you bring up him killing your father?"

He was right. Riordan was suspected of at least half a dozen murders but had never been arrested for one.

"I don't have a choice. This might be my only chance to find out what really happened." I stood up to leave. "And who might have been responsible."

Riordan lived in a dumpy studio apartment on Brighton Street. I thought an in-demand hitman might have classier digs. I knocked on the door and got no answer.

As I drove home, my cell rang. The caller ID read Colleen Sheehan. We had been seeing each other for a year and I teetered on the edge of doing something I had never done before—falling in love. I had met her at a southside party, and we hit it off right away. Her hair was the shade of orange at sunset and her eyes as green as spring in Ireland. She was a second-grade teacher, and she had a sweet and caring way about her.

"Hi," she said. "Thought you might want me to cook you dinner tonight."

"Just what I was hoping. Nothing I would like better. I'll be home in ten."

"See you there," she said before ending the call.

She knocked on the door minutes after I arrived. She carried a couple of shopping bags and a small overnight bag.

"I'm getting more than dinner?"

"Play your cards right and you might," she said.

I put a Van Morrison CD on the stereo. "I'm going to take a quick shower."

When I came back to the kitchen, she handed me a glass of Napa Valley cab. Water for pasta was boiling and she was making a salad. I set the table, and we ate.

I told her about my meeting with Flynn and that I had tried to find Riordan. She didn't say much except, "Why are Irish boys always so quick to use their fists? There would be much less trouble in this town if that weren't the case."

We finished the wine, I did the dishes, and we went to bed. We had just finished making love when police kicked in the door.

"What the hell?" I said as two plainclothes cops entered the bedroom.

"We have a warrant," one of them replied.

I got up, grabbing a pair of sweats. Two uniforms were tearing apart the living room. Two more were tossing the kitchen. One of them pulled a bag from under the sink and said "Sarge, got something."

One of the detectives came in and examined the contents.

"Cuff him," he said. "Patrick Flaherty, you're under arrest for possession of cocaine and the murder of Daniel Riordan."

* * *

I sat in an interrogation room trying to make sense of what the hell was going on. Two detectives played good cop, bad cop with me. The older of the two was short and squat. His tie was loosened and there were rings of sweat under his arms.

"Look Patrick, I understand. Guy whacks your old man, and robs you of your father. You've been carrying that around for years. It eats at you. You think you aren't much of a son if you don't take revenge and kill the bastard when an opportunity comes along. Who could blame you?"

I didn't respond.

The other guy took a run at me. He was younger, a slick looking guy. Nice suit, fancy haircut. He played the bad cop role—and did it pretty damned convincingly.

"A kilo of coke Flaherty. That'll get ya life in this state. Is that why you murdered Riordan? To steal the blow? Maybe shooting him had nothing to do with your old man. Way I hear it, he was a loser too." He walked around the room for a minute. "Riordan was shot three times. The revolver we found in your apartment had three shells left. Ballistics will show it's the murder weapon. We find your prints on it, and you'll fry like Sunday chicken."

I tried to stay calm. I tried to act like they hadn't rattled me. But to tell the truth, I had never been so scared. I knew what I was up against— a classic Southside setup. And I wasn't sure I could get out of it.

"I want my lawyer."

Quinn arrived half an hour later.

"Sorry if I woke you," I said. "I'm scared, Mike. I know Flynn is behind this. What I don't know is if it's because I decked him or if I got too close to what happened to my father. Maybe both."

He put his hand on my shoulder. "Don't worry, Pat. We'll get you out of this. You'll be arraigned in the morning, bail will be set, and we'll go from there. Who could have gotten into your place?"

"Just Colleen. She was there tonight when they busted in."

He cocked an eyebrow but didn't say anything.

A jail guard arrived to take me to a holding cell.

"See you in the morning," Mike said as I was led away.

I didn't sleep. Either the cops planted the gun and the drugs or Colleen did. I didn't believe it could have been her. Flynn had to have bribed the cops. It had happened before, that's how the game was played on the southside. I spent most of the night worrying about what might happen. I knew my prints weren't on the gun so the murder charge might not stick, but the coke was another story.

My arraignment was at ten. Mike came to my cell at 9:45. "Got bad news, Patrick. Colleen wasn't home and she wasn't at school. And Miles Jordan is the judge who will be hearing your case. There have been rumors about Flynn's relationship with him."

My spirits were low as I entered the courtroom. Jordan was about seventy, overweight, and slovenly. He had unruly gray hair that looked like it hadn't been cut in a while. A pair of wire-rimmed glasses hung crookedly on his nose.

"Patrick Flaherty, how do you plead to the charges of pre-meditated murder in the first degree and possession of cocaine with intent to distribute?"

"Not guilty, your honor," I said.

"Bail is set at two million dollars." He banged his gavel, and I was taken back to a cell.

My mother and aunt Sheila put their homes up as collateral, and I was released later that day. The trial date was set to begin in just under a month. I was placed on administrative leave from the planning commission and the vote on Flynn's project was put on hold. I started drinking more than I should have—partly to pass the time but mostly to quell my fear. I didn't think I could survive prison.

Mike came to see me one morning a week before the trial was to start. I was already drunk. "Wanna beer?" I offered.

He shook his head. "Get your shit together, Patrick. You look like crap. You don't want a jury to see you looking like that."

"It doesn't matter, Mike. Flynn's gonna screw me. He'll use me to prove things will never change on the southside. It's the same old story. The same way it's always been."

"I have some news for you. Colleen deposited twenty-five thousand dollars three days after you were arrested. But she's in the wind. I have two private dicks trying to track her down. We have a lead that she's in Florida. But here's the thing, it's enough to establish doubt to a jury. The ballistics came back and your prints weren't on the gun. I'm feeling better about this even with Jordan as the judge. And yeah, I'll have a beer."

The day before the trial, Colleen was served a subpoena in Miami. She would have to testify. I started to think this nightmare might end.

On the first day of the trial, the prosecution laid out their case against me. The District Attorney who was running for re-election and endorsed by Flynn would be trying the case. I watched the reaction of the jurors and had to admit that the evidence was starting to sound weak.

Colleen was in court the second day and, after Mike told the jurors what a sham the trial was, he called her to the stand.

"Miss Sheehan, were you at Mr. Flaherty's the night he was arrested?"

She nodded her head and said, "Yes."

"And did you plant the .38 revolver and a kilogram of cocaine in Mr. Flaherty's apartment that night?"

"No, I did not. Why would I do such a thing? We were falling in love."

"Isn't it true that before today you hadn't seen him since the night of his arrest and that three days later you deposited twenty-five thousand dollars in a checking account and fled to Florida? And isn't it also true that you were staying in a condo in Miami Beach owned by Kevin Flynn? Let me remind you, Miss Sheehan, that you are under oath."

She started to sob. "Lefty Shannon is my Godfather. Flynn threatened to kill him if I didn't go along. He said he'd kill me too. I told Lefty about it. He felt bad about what might happen to Patrick. He also told me Flynn had Patrick's father killed when the Patriots won their first Super Bowl. Lefty was the bookie, but Flynn's cash was behind him, and Patrick's father won fifty thousand dollars on the game. When Flynn wouldn't pay, Mr. Flaherty beat him up. Flynn hired Riordan to kill him. I'm so sorry Patrick, I didn't mean for this to happen or to hurt you. I hope somehow you can forgive me."

Mike's motion for a mistrial was granted even though Judge Jordan didn't look happy about it. When the police went to arrest Flynn for Riordan's murder and arranging my father's death, he put a bullet in his head.

I celebrated with Mike that night. Big steaks and shots of Jameson. I raised a toast.

"It's been the same old story on the southside for far too long. Here's to a new story. Hopefully one with a happier ending."

"I'll drink to that," Mike said.

And we did.

Round and Round

(From the album, Toys in the Attic)

Eve Fisher

Mildred showed up at one of the music rehearsals for the annual prison St. Dysmas Christmas Pageant. My cellie Doc, who plays bass, happened to look up during a guitar riff and saw a woman standing in the picture window in the classroom above the chapel. He dropped his pick and pointed, croaking, "Mildred!"

The whole band—all inmates, except for the guest singer from one of the local churches—looked up.

"Holy shit!" Smiler cried out before clapping his hand over his mouth.

The few inmates watching the show—including me—craned our necks, and by God, it sure looked like her. You couldn't see her face, but the outline was right: hair in a bun, wearing a Depression-era-style dress with a white collar. Not that we'd ever seen a picture of her, but it fits the other sightings.

And then she vanished. Just the way she always does.

The outsiders stared at each other, then us, then back at each other, and you could tell they were wondering if they should run for the hills before we all launched a riot and a prison break.

Pastor Whitemead got up and said, "All right, back to rehearsals. Christmas is only a couple of weeks away."

One of the outside guests said, "What's going on, Rick?"

"I'll explain later. We've only got fifteen minutes left—"

Meanwhile, I was looking around for Officer Corvo, but he wasn't in the chapel. Probably up in the COs office, watching us on camera.

And sure enough, Corvo came walking in a moment later, after the music started again. I met him at the door, and he asked, "What's the matter, Bell?"

"Mildred in the Upper Classroom."

"Really?"

"Really. Ask Pastor Whitemead. He'll tell you the same."

By now Whitemead had come up to us. He confirmed what I said and asked, "Maybe you could check the surveillance cameras?"

"There aren't any cameras behind the stage or in the upper classrooms," Corvo replied. "We keep trying to get them, but the DOC vetoes it every time. Too much money." Whitemead shook his head. "If it's any comfort, it's not your imagination. Most of us have seen her." Then he called out to us inmates, *"Count!"*

* * *

Mildred is our penitentiary ghost. Back in 1925, she was a farmer's wife who ran off from her husband, William (never "Bill") Ehler, with her high school sweetheart Earl Wilson. I reckon Earl was wild, because her parents nipped it in the bud and somehow got her to marry not-wild William. But raising three kids on a flat quarter section of land, two hours from town even with a Model T seems to have palled on her. When Earl showed up at the farm, it didn't take him long to sweet-talk her into running off with him. Without the kids, of course. And everything changed, nothing stayed the same after that. Went on a short crime spree that ended up in Flandreau, staying above their means at the Calumet Hotel, which is still in business, and apparently haunted, but not by Mildred.

Earl and Mildred were arrested, tried, and convicted, and because there was only one penitentiary in South Dakota in those days, in Sioux Falls, that's where they both went. The women's prison was an attachment to the Warden's house, and there should have been no contact. But love finds a way and they manage to exchange notes. A couple of years down the road one of those notes from Earl told her to come to what was then the infirmary but is now somewhere in the chapel. She did. I don't know what she was expecting—my bet is an escape plan or a quick smooch and cuddle—but no, he stabbed her to death.

And she's still there.

* * *

Well, word spread like wildfire—every sighting of Mildred does—and people went nuts. A blaze of dreams, and no one was sure if they weren't someone else's.

Norte, enforcer for the Latin Kings, dreamed he was driving his old lowrider Impala, when he heard something knocking the trunk—so he stopped in the middle lane to go open it, but the closer he got, the more he knew it was *her* and he didn't dare open it… "And sure enough, the next day, I heard from my cousin that some bastard stole my Impala from the garage. What the hell does she want with my *car*?"

Old Thunder dreamed he was at the mall, looking at an apocalyptic sky, with a bunch of people who were talking about the end of the world. Someone said, "Maybe we're already dead," and he asked, "Well, how would we know?" The same person said, "We could rise up to heaven." So, they all held hands in a circle and started going up in the air, and he looked at the person who started it all and knew it was *her*… And came crashing back down, awake, heart thudding in his bunk.

Doc and I work in the infirmary, so I was there when he came to plead with Lydia, our Nurse Practitioner, for an EKG or at least to listen to his heart. "I might be dying!"

"Doubtful," Lydia replied, but she got out her stethoscope and listened. "Everything's fine."

"But my heart's pounding!"

"That's 'cause you're scaring yourself to death. Calm down."

"Can you give me a valium?" Thunder asked.

"Nice try," Lydia said. She turned to our LPN Diane and said, "Give him two Tylenol." Then she turned back to Thunder, "And we shouldn't do that."

Meanwhile, Forrest, our janitor and general go-fer for the infirmary, would not leave or go anywhere alone, because Mildred might be waiting for him.

"Now, Forrest," I said, "she never does anyone any harm. She just gets lonely, that's all."

"Sh-sh-she's dead," Forrest replied. "She sh-sh-shouldn't be around at all."

"Don't worry," Lydia said. "Bell and I won't let her do anything to you."

"Th-that's why I'm not going anywhere. I'm safe here."

Coyote's cousin Bordeaux told everyone that, when he and the Native American group were drum practicing Tuesday night for the upcoming powwow, he looked up, and saw a woman staring in the window at them. Mildred, of course. So Coyote, who's the prison medicine man, told them they needed to have a special sage ceremony, just to be careful. And hard-ass Lieutenant Davis didn't laugh but gave permission. They ended up having it in the gym, and they drew quite a crowd.

Standing in the Great Circle, waiting for my turn, I saw officers, staff, and inmates from every unit. Even shot callers, enforcers, and members of different gangs, got saged and didn't even glare at each other. They might not believe in much, but everybody believed in Mildred.

Okay, Cuete and Bowie glared, but what else can you expect from rival drug dealers? Only that morning I'd personally watched Cuete stick out a leg and trip Bowie, who instantly got back on his feet and turned around, ready to pop him. Officer Olson jumped in and separated them—and then wrote up *Bowie* for the violation. Cuete sauntered on while Bowie cussed a blue streak (and got another write-up). Why? Hell if I know. Maybe Olson hadn't gotten his cut that week, or he just didn't like Bowie. Anything is possible. Olson's a real dick, and I'd often wondered how he got such a lovely wife as our LPN Diane.

Meanwhile, drug use was up all over the prison, which is one way inmates avoid stress and celebrate holidays in prison. (Doc and I stick to his hooch.) These days, most drugs come in as paper soaked in K-2, etc., and dried. The administration always says that it's visitors and volunteers who bring drugs in, but we know it's (some) officers and staff who do it for money. Like Olson. The gangs all have contacts out on the street who are still running the business while their shot callers are inside. Money's provided, the paper comes in, and it's distributed more or less discreetly. Janitors get a taste of both the money and the drugs for their cooperation. A lot of trash doesn't have that much trash in it, if you know what I mean, and it only got worse when the DOC decided everyone was gonna recycle. Smiler, who knows everything, says the recycling bins were a great boon to the internal drug trade. Round and round, into the bins and out again.

* * *

Going back to Officer Olson, I'd also wondered if he was the same at home as at work. I'd like to think not, but… His wife was younger than he was, I don't how much. Been in here too long to know how people age outside. Nice looking, but her real asset was her compassion (an asset lacking in some staff). And she'd always had a cheerful disposition, but over the last couple of years that had gone from natural to something she put on, like her makeup. And some of that makeup hid bruises. She spent a lot of time talking with Lydia in her office, and they rarely laughed.

It was a few days after the sage ceremony that Diane didn't come into work. And the next day Lydia told us she was taking medical leave. She'd had an accident, fallen down the stairs, and broken her arm.

"She'll be back soon," Lydia said, but grimly.

"Let her know we're all thinking about her," I said.

* * *

"Some men should not be allowed to get married," I told Doc at rec a week later. Diane was still on medical leave, and Lydia's mood was sour.

"We don't know that he did anything to her. She could have tripped."

"You sunshine patriot," I said. "You know what an asshole Olson is."

"Yeah, but—"

"Hey, guys," Bowie said, sitting down with us, breathless and sweaty from pumping iron.

"Bowie," I said politely.

"Uh, look, I just wanted to ask—what happened to Mrs. Olson?"

"She's on sick leave," I said. "Didn't you hear?"

"Been in the SHU," Bowie replied. "Olson gave me another write-

21

up, three in three days, and I just got out. Catchin' up ever since. She gonna be okay? What's wrong with her?"

"Just an accident," Doc said. "Broke her arm."

Bowie's face flushed. "She gonna be all right?"

"As far as we know." I glanced at Doc, who got up saying, "I'm going to get some pop."

After Doc left, I leaned in and asked, "Why do you care?"

"Because…" Bowie looked around. "You know the way Olson's got it in for me? Writing me up all the time?"

"Yeah."

"I think she told him something she shouldn't have."

He was looking me straight in the eyes, with no shiftiness, just concern.

"You and her?" He nodded. "When?"

"Last year, when I was out on parole for a while."

"Jesus," I said. I believed him. Bowie is young, well-spoken when he wants to be, and almost unbelievably good looking. If it weren't for his drug dealing, drug habit, and a tendency to boost the occasional car, he could make a good living as a model.

"Where the hell did you run into each other?"

"Starbucks." He glanced around and then lowered his head even more. "Look, it just happened. She just sent me spinning… It was like my feet never touched the ground when I was around her. After a while, she got the guilts and broke it off. But… I still care about her. I really do. I think… Maybe if she hadn't ended it, I might have stayed out, just for her."

"Pretty to think so," I said, but he'd never heard that line. "So you think he knows."

Bowie nodded. "And he's a major control freak. That's why she's working here, so he knows where she is all the time. She could make better money almost anywhere else. And you wouldn't believe what she had to do so we could see each other—"

"I don't want to know. But I believe you. I believe you."

"Is there any way to stop him?" Bowie asked. "After this—"

I'd been keeping an eye on the window and saw Olson walking down the hallway.

"Shut up and get up. Olson's coming. I'll talk to you at another time."

And Bowie was across the room in a flash, joking around with the Wiccans.

* * *

That night in our cell, I whispered it all to Doc. "So, he's playing with Bowie, like a cat with a mouse. And with Diane. What a shit."

"She had an affair. Some people would say she's lucky to be alive," said Doc, who was in prison for killing his wife.

"What's wrong with divorce?" I asked.

"If you'd ever been married, you'd understand."

"Not my fault. All the women I asked to marry me were smart enough to say no. We've got to do something."

"Like what?" Doc asked. "I am not going to death row, even for Miss Olson."

"The problem with you is that you always think the worst," I complained. "I'm thinking more in terms of Mildred. I think she certainly would understand the situation Diane's in. Everything changes, but it's really the same damn bullshit over and over again. And I doubt she has much use for Olson. I think she'd be willing to help us out."

"How are you going to get Mildred to take care of Olson?" Doc asked. "Hold a séance?"

"Wouldn't hurt," I replied. "I'm sure one of the Wiccans would host."

"Of all the lunatics in all the prisons in the world, I end up with you," Doc said, sighing. "I'll ask Payday."

* * *

Payday, who's devout, liked the idea of a séance and sold it to the officers in charge as an attempt to lay Mildred to rest. Or at least get her to give us a break over the holidays. Despite a couple of snickers, even they thought it was a pretty good idea.

"Might quiet everyone down," Lieutenant Davis said.

"Exactly," Payday replied. "Everyone's on edge. We need to do something about it so we can all celebrate the holidays right. This'll make the guys feel better."

We met in the rec room before open rec started. Payday, Doc, Smiler, Bowie, and Coyote, who had his own reasons for hating Olson. We held hands, leaned in, and started whispering.

"It's got to be during a St. Dysmas service when Olson's working it," I said.

"I'll get the schedule," Payday said.

"Smiler, we're going to need you to get the stairs prepped *after* everybody's in."

"I'm on it," Smiler replied.

"How are we going to get Olson to come down?" Doc asked.

"I'll lead a Native American protest against the imperialism of American Christmas," Coyote said. "If that doesn't bring him down, nothing will."

"And I'll be waiting at the very bottom," Bowie said, "dressed as Mildred." We all stared at him. "I've done it before," Bowie said. "Corvo likes to play Mildred pranks on people."

"Like a few weeks ago?" I asked. "That was you?"

"I've got to have *one* officer on my side," Bowie replied.

"What, he's got a dress—"

"And a wig stashed," Bowie said. "And no, I'm not telling you where. Just roll with it, okay?"

"Okay, okay."

And at the end of the séance, we all sang "Auld Lang Syne," asked Mildred for her help, and assured her that we would never forget her.

* * *

It really did all go like clockwork.

Olson went upstairs.

Smiler ran up to ask him if he wanted some cookies during coffee time. Then he came back down, gave us the nod, and sat back down.

The service started, and after about fifteen minutes, Coyote and a handful of Native Americans marched down, carrying homemade signs that basically said, "Keep the Crap out of Christmas," chanting as they went.

Pastor Whitemead finally got them to shut up, and that's when we heard the screams.

"What in the world—"

Pastor Whitemead headed for the door, and everyone followed. Out on the landing—there were two flights of stairs from the entrance to the chapel, with another shorter flight above that, each with its own landing—was a sign "Slippery When Wet."

By then the screams had stopped, and Olson was at the very bottom. His neck was twisted too far for comfort, and his legs like looked the old Raggedy Andy dolls they sold when I was a boy. Officers came running from the control pod, and I knew what was coming next. Code Red. And then *every* officer on deck came, we were all sent back upstairs, and were on lockdown until about eleven that night.

More than one officer later swore that before he died, Olson said "Mildred."

Whew. Took a lot of hooch to get to sleep that night.

Now here's the weird part:

Bowie never made it to the chapel area to play his part. He was back in the SHU, sent there by Olson for some reason or other that very afternoon.

So, I reckon Mildred really didn't like Olson, either.

Oh, and no one saw her again until the February full moon. But that's another story.

Last Child

(From the album, Rocks)
Avram Lavinsky

His ears still ringing with the hypnotic rhythm of the machinery at the plant, Macaulay Keating swallowed down the last of his Pabst Blue Ribbon draft. He nodded as the bartender whisked away his empty glass, and a moment later, another, identical to the first, replaced it. His stool at the Snug Harbor Alehouse felt more like home than his little studio apartment on Deaver Street, though not quite as homelike as the dreamy memories of his grade-school years in a handful of towns along the Florida panhandle.

From the corner of the bar came the unmistakable sharp clack of the break in a game of eight ball followed by the low syncopated thuds of two balls falling into pockets and a deep satisfied grunt from Kage. Perennially unemployed and content to sleep in until the early afternoon, Kage always had far more energy on nights out, but Mac had long since given up on suggesting job opportunities to his older half-brother. No, Kage wouldn't change. He would remain a committer of petty crimes and a dreamer of grand ones. Mac could only hope that his brother never had the guts or the stupidity to carry out schemes like the one he'd been spouting off about this week.

Mac lifted his head to sneak a look at the stranger on the second stool to his right. There was no doubt the mud-covered Porche in the lot belonged to the young man. Aside from the fact that Mac knew every crappy vehicle belonging to every regular at Snug Harbor, the stranger seemed to match the car. His wrinkled Members Only jacket had a small, blackened hole in one sleeve, a burn from some wayward ash.

The lenses of his Ray-Ban sunglasses, folded on the thickly polyurethaned hardwood bar top, showed scuffs and scratches, even in the dim lighting. Everything about him told of careless and neglectful wealth.

Around the corner of the bar, Tina seemed aware of the stranger as well. She fidgeted, folding and unfolding her arms over her tank top, the smooth skin of her shoulders catching the beam of the pendant light. She shot nervous and expectant smiles in the general direction of the stranger, rotating her pilsner glass. It had remained a third full for some time, as if inviting him to buy her the next round.

Raised voices at the pool table caught the stranger's attention. Kage was leaning over his opponent menacingly, spittle flying from his mouth, as the two argued over whether they'd agreed to play ball-in-pocket rules. Six years older, four inches taller, and sixty pounds heavier than Mac, Kage often took on the feral look of a crazed mountain man when angered.

As the stranger turned his head to glance at the raised voices, Mac caught a glimpse of his face beyond the mousey-brown waves of his hair, the something familiar in the rounded contour of his nose.

"C.J.?"

C.J. looked up at Mac, awkwardly at first. Then, he smiled with recognition. "From Morgan's Cove. Mac, right?"

"Yeah!" Mac leaned over to clap C.J. on the shoulder.

Morgan's Cove, September 14, 1981. The high point of Mac's years in Worcester. Maybe that wasn't saying much.

When his mother's reputation among Florida landlords began to follow her, she had loaded the family into the Malibu wagon and driven to North Carolina. Eventually, they worked their way north to New England, and his mom had decided on Worcester after checking Boston rents in the *Want Ad Digest*.

Even the first time they pulled off I-290, Mac could sense the medieval air of a city in decline: the wide streets with little traffic, the boarded-up businesses, the empty factories.

Then, last summer, came the rumor. The Rolling Stones were staying right here in Worcester County, rehearsing and recording at a studio in North Brookfield.

And then, on a Monday night, Kage had rushed into Snugs and dragged Mac off this very same stool because the Stones were playing just a quarter mile away at Sir Morgan's Cove.

By the time they arrived, the street outside was rocking, the mob stretching on for blocks, the air electric. Kage bulldozed his way through the jam-packed bodies in the parking lot, pulling Mac with him, until they reached one of a few dozen helmeted police officers holding back the deluge of humanity, thousands of rabid Stones fans, demanding entrance into a space that could only possibly hold one tenth of them…or maybe one twentieth going by the fire code. All the while, beneath the shouts, the muffled pulse of the bass, and the kick drum rattled the emergency exits and vibrated Mac's belly.

Then, with a loud click and a metallic groan, someone popped open a fire door from within, and a violent surge in the sea of bodies swept Mac forward. The crushing force of the stampede pinned him against a cop's shoulder. The eyes of the two men locked in mutual terror for one endless moment, the handle of the cop's baton held in his tightly clenched fist even as bodies pressing from every direction left him no room to swing it.

And then, in a rush of wind, the cop and the night air and gravity all disappeared. The wave of fans carried Mac into the room, and the fire door clicked closed.

He was inside, bodies writhing in rhythm to "Gimme Shelter" all around him like the legs of an enormous millipede, all pressed so tightly together that he believed he could feel the synchronized pulsing of their arteries. He caught glimpses of Mick Jagger and Ron Wood on the stage, their faces ethereal and wraithlike in the colored lights. Across the room, the taps flowed nonstop as bartenders snatched bills and raced to pass drinks into waiting hands.

A door set back alongside the stage opened. A young man emerged, unruly waves of hair barely touching his shoulder as he nodded to the music. He seemed from another universe…or perhaps native to this strange other universe that the night belonged to. As the crowd engulfed him, he seemed somehow immune to their manic euphoria, whether through habitual exposure to it or the dark influence of some greater power.

Then, taken by a strange eddy within the undulating bodies, Mac found himself next to him. The boy was holding a shiny metal pipe, the turned-up bulbous end already stuffed with a partially crumpled green bud. A gold lighter sparked. The bud glowed orange for a few seconds, and he offered Mac a toke.

"You guys know each other?" Tina had left her seat and drifted toward them. She smiled invitingly at C.J.

"We met at the Stones show," said Mac.

"God." Tina pouted. "Everybody but me got in."

"He wasn't just *in*," said Mac. "He was *backstage*."

All eyes were now on C.J.

Kage lumbered toward them, his pool game either decided or no longer of interest.

C.J. shrugged awkwardly. "My dad parties with them sometimes."

"No shit!" Kage's bear-like form hovered at his side. "How cool is that?"

C.J.'s shoulders lifted nearly to his ears.

Kage drew closer, despite the smaller man's discomfort. "Kage Keating." He offered his hand.

"C.J. Elliot."

Kage's hand swallowed C.J.'s and shook it with a single downward thrust. "Wait. You're not, like, a son or a grandson of Cameron James Elliot, are you?"

C.J. squirmed. "Grandson."

"The Elliot family," said Kage, seeing Mac's lack of comprehension, "they own that company…Allegiance Investments."

Mac had heard of Allegiance. At the shoe factory, they encouraged him to put money in an Allegiance mutual fund for his retirement. They would even match him up to a certain amount. Of course, he'd never managed to put away a single dime, not after the state and federal government carved their greedy share out of his paycheck, but someday he would. He'd also seen commercials for Allegiance Investments on TV. Somehow, it had never occurred to him that the giant company might be family-owned.

"The employees own the majority of it," said C.J., as if hearing Mac's thoughts. "That's what everybody loves to say. The family owns forty-nine percent, and my grandfather owns most of that."

"Ain't that something." Kage's slightly bloodshot eyes widened. A bit of spattle from his earlier argument clung to the inside edge of his scraggly beard. "Do you have, like, your own island or something?"

"I wish," said C.J., sounding disarmed by Kage's directness but still holding his shoulders stiffly up near his ears. "My granddad's always been a bit of a miser. I think he used to really care for me. I'm my dad's youngest and the last grandchild, but he doesn't like my dad's partying. Or mine. He's more-or-less cut us off."

"That's awful," said Tina, shaking out her puffed-up hair and staring into C.J.'s eyes until he looked up at her.

"I always joke that the only way to get Gramps to share the wealth would be to have myself kidnapped and get a ransom."

In the corner beyond the pool table, a glass shattered against the floor, the impact high-pitched and percussive.

The plastic grins on the faces of Kage and Tina remained unchanged.

"Let me buy you a drink," said Mac. "I owe you one from that night at Sir Morgan's. Actually, I owe you a few."

With each round of drinks, C.J.'s awkwardness lifted noticeably, and the space between him and Tina slowly evaporated. Her gesticulations slowly began to include playful pats on the denim along his thigh, then more lingering caresses of his forearm.

"Where can we light up around here?" he asked.

"We usually just use the back of my van," said Kage. "Cops don't come around back much."

Twenty minutes later, the side door of the van slid open, and thick, sweet smoke dissipated in the mist beneath the parking lot's only streetlamp. As the two brothers climbed out and disappeared in the direction of the bar's back entrance, Tina and C.J. sat shoulder to shoulder on the edge of the van's floor with their feet on the asphalt.

When their hands intertwined, Tina's grin widened, her eyes tranquil and triumphant behind half-closed lids.

Slouching as if he could barely keep himself upright, C.J. turned to her and gripped her head in both his hands. He clumsily brought his face to hers and nudged her parted lips with his. Then he drew back a few inches.

Tina's grin remained, and her eyes stared unflinchingly into his face, even as the shadow fell over them both.

Kage's enormous hand clamped across C.J.'s mouth as his other forearm wrapped over his throat. He swung C.J. halfway out and then slammed him to the metal floor.

C.J. thrashed feebly as if in a nightmare.

Tina produced a roll of duct tape from under the passenger seat.

C.J. managed a stifled yell, but an instant later, Kage wrapped the tape across his mouth all the way around the nape of his neck and doubled it over.

A first zip tie dug into his wrists and locked his hands together behind his back. A second bound his ankles together, and Kage wrenched his shins up to force a third around the other two, hog-tying him.

"That was no act." Kage rose to his knees and snarled at Tina. "You're really into him, aren't you?"

"Not my type." She put her palms below the collar of Kage's T-shirt. "Guys like him never figure out what I like. You know that."

He grabbed a fistful of her hair and yanked her head back. The two locked in a wide-mouthed kiss.

"Roll him to his side." Mac leaned in for a better view of C.J.'s prone form.

"What you like is money," said Kage to Tina, ignoring his brother. "It gets you going, don't it?"

"When this is all over and we get what's coming to us," she said, "we'll find out, won't we?"

"God," said Mac, leaning in and seeing C.J.'s beet-red face, "he can't breathe." He climbed around them, rolled C.J. onto his side facing the door, and shifted a length of duct tape that had covered one of his nostrils. "I don't get it. This isn't what you two talked about."

"This is *exactly* what we talked about," said Kage.

"You just said you wanted to grab some banker and get a ransom out of the spouse."

"And the man upstairs heard us and sent us the motherload of all banking families. Billions. They have billions. He practically told us himself we should kidnap him. We score this one, we'll have the whole city at our feet."

"But he's seen all our faces," said Mac. "How do you plan on getting around that?"

"I must have put twenty grams in his drinks all told," said Kage. "He ain't gonna remember much."

Wanting to believe this, Mac looked into his brother's dark eyes for a few long seconds but saw only predatory hunger there. He left the van, keenly aware of an unstoppable force propelling him toward a collision with his brother, like the shifting plates beneath two continents.

* * *

Mac cut the engine to his Honda CB550, climbed off the bike, slipped his helmet off, and hung it off one handlebar. The top edge of a rusted snowplow rose above the knee-high sedges in the meadow. He headed past the collapsing stable with its near wall folded in. Where the doors should have hung, tall ferns and sassafras crowded the entrance. Inside, an old Willys Mechanical Mule platform truck sat at an odd angle, the cargo bed strewn with rotting bark from hauling firewood.

Kage's van stood by the abandoned farmhouse. As Mac climbed down the bulkhead stairs to the basement, an unexpected smell mingled with the odors of mildew, stale beer, and sweat: the scent of cooked beef. Kage was sitting at an old wooden chair and school desk, using a hunting knife to cut up what had to be five or six pounds of recently cooked sirloin steak, a row of empty forty-ounce bottles at his feet.

Beyond him, Tina had passed out, her cheek on a similar desktop in a puddle of beer.

A house sparrow that had been trapped in the dank space since Saturday hopped onto the corner of Kage's desk.

"Damn rat with wings." He swatted at it with the knife.

It fluttered away into a shadowy corner.

Kage rose to pursue it, his chair scraping against the concrete floor.

"Don't hurt it," said C.J., only his bottom lip visible beneath his makeshift hood. "Please."

"Leave it." Mac understood how much C.J. needed the little bird. Hours of solitude could be just as devastating as physical deprivation. He eyed the steak suspiciously. "What are you doing? What's going on here?"

"God," said Kage sawing off a long strip of meat, "First you bitch and moan that we're not feeding him enough, and now you bitch and moan that we're feeding him."

As Mac's eyes adjusted to the dim light from the filthy and cracked half windows at ground level, he caught the glimmer of something new leaning against the stone wall. A bolt cutter.

He looked from the tool to C.J. and the rusty chain running from his neck to the giant waste main running vertically behind him. "What are you going to do?"

"We're going to feed our guest," said Kage. "And if you don't like the way we're handling things, keep in mind, you don't have to be a part of this."

"It's been five days," said Mac. "If the family was going to pay, they'd have done it by now."

"See now, if you'd done any of the real work around here, you'd know the latest from C.J.'s mom and the Elliots. They're gonna pay. They just want proof that we're serious and C.J. over there is alive."

"Kage…what are you planning to do with that bolt cutter?"

"Prob'ly start with a pinky. Think I might just send it off US mail, regular delivery…unless you feel like springing for overnight."

"How do you get your money if he bleeds out?"

"That's what the extra iron in his dinner's for. I think we can manage to tie him off. Can't be that complicated."

"It's filthy down here. It'll get infected. I'm not letting you murder him."

"Time for you to go Macky-boy. You're not needed here."

Mac considered, the blood pounding in his ears. He started toward the bolt cutter and only sensed his brother flying at him just in time to square off.

The two grappled. They locked in a clinch like two praying mantises.

Then they toppled. Mac's skull slammed into the concrete floor.

Kage rained down blows on him, straddling him. "Always the same! Always too damn good for everyone! Always the sweet baby of the family."

Mac pulled his forearms up to shield his face. A savage blow to his ear left his head ringing.

The torrent of words spewed on, Kage beating Mac's head like a bass drum, marking words for emphasis. "All the *times* I took a *whoop*-ing for your *bull*-shit, every bag of *dope* that was *yours* and not *mine!*"

Mac twisted violently.

They rolled.

He found himself teetering atop his brother's body, but then they rolled again.

The legs of the desk scraped against the floor. The plate smashed.

Kage's giant fist came down upon Mac's temple, driving his head sideways into the concrete.

The world seemed to jerk and bounce. It blurred. It darkened at the edges.

A moment later…or maybe an hour later, from far off, Mac heard a faltering voice. He tried to respond but found he couldn't inhale. A weight pressed against his chest.

"I'm sorry," said C.J. "I'm so sorry."

Something wet mixed with the grit of the basement floor. Mac's eyelids lifted. A giant, lifeless, dark eye stared back at him…through him. He jerked frantically until his brother's body slid off his chest. He scrambled back and sat up against the rough stones of a wall.

Kage lay on his belly, his head at a strange angle like the cab of a jackknifed tractor-trailer. The handle of the hunting knife protruded from the base of his neck.

"Oh God." Mac jerked to one side, sure he would vomit. He gagged, but nothing came up.

C.J. held his blood-covered right hand over his heart. "I'm so sorry. He was going to kill me. I'm sure of it. I could see it in his eyes. You knew. You saw it. I know you did."

Mac hugged his knees to his chest. He nodded. Yes. Yes, Kage would have killed C.J. He would have killed him without a thought. All for some fat stack of paper notes that he thought would make him a better man even though it would only stick in his throat and choke out whatever humanity remained in him.

Tina sniffled and muttered something unintelligible, rocking her head on the desk before settling into silence once again.

Convulsing with silent sobs, Mac went to his brother's body, nearly gagging once again at the metallic smell of blood. He rolled Kage to his side and searched his hip pockets. Finding the small key, he staggered to C.J., unlocked the padlock, and removed his chains. "What do we do now?"

"I don't care what happens," said C.J. "You can cut off my pinky and get the money if you want to. Nothing matters to me. I'm just so sorry."

"But *right now*. What do we do?"

For a long time, the two men listened to Tina's slow rhythmic breathing, interrupted only by an occasional doubled chirp from the house sparrow.

"I guess," said C.J., "there is one thing that matters to me."

It took the two nearly half an hour to coax the bird out the bulkhead door by swinging Mac's sweatshirt in its direction, C.J. pleading caution with each attempt. Finally, it glided into the light of the setting sun and rose out of sight.

Sight for Sore Eyes
(From the album, Draw the Line)
John C. Bruening

Joey's shoulder hurt like a son of a bitch. Even the smallest movement, the slightest shift of his weight in the metal folding chair, sent sharp stabs of pain down the length of his arm.

Just getting from the street and into his building, and then up the flight of stairs and into his apartment, had been a monumental struggle. Along the way, the pain had been enough to make him think he might pass out.

He'd found an old leather belt in his dresser and fashioned it into a makeshift sling. Getting his arm into it had been a nightmare all its own, but he'd immobilized it enough to keep at least some of the pain under control.

He wiped the sweat from his face with his good hand. Even that simple motion made him gasp as another stab of pain burned through the opposite shoulder.

He could barely move. How the hell was he going to play?

His eyes settled on the guitar case and the Fender amp on the floor in the corner of the room. He'd been with Water on the Sun for about a year and a half. He'd been playing guitar for several years before that, but Water on the Sun needed a bass player, and he needed the steady gig. So, he agreed to step into the background and hold down the bottom for everyone else.

He'd been a little resentful about it at first, but not for long. Water on the Sun got traction quickly, selling out local venues and then gaining a consistent following throughout western Pennsylvania and even parts of Ohio. And once he and Sarah, the lead singer, acknowledged their unmistakable connection—onstage and off—the whole thing felt effortless.

She had a voice like an angel. There was no denying it. They were all excellent musicians, but everyone knew she was the secret ingredient, the natural center of the vortex. If they were going to get to the next level, she would be the ticket. She had the stuff—not just the voice but the presence—that could take them all the way.

He picked up the phone and dialed. Just hearing her voice would help. It always did. Hell, her voice made everyone feel good. Hundreds of people at a time. Why should he be different? And then she'd come over and they'd make some kind of plan to get him to a hospital and get him fixed.

Joey heard three rings on the other end of the line before Sarah picked up. "Hello?"

"Baby, it's me."

"Joey?" The question sounded odd, like she needed to confirm his identity.

"Yeah," he said.

"What's going on?"

"I got a problem."

"What is it?"

"There was an accident."

"Are you okay?"

"I don't know," said Joey. "It's my shoulder."

"What happened?"

"Some asshole almost ran me over."

"What?"

"I was downtown. I stepped off the curb and this car came out of nowhere. I jumped out of the way, but I tripped on the curb and came down hard, and now my shoulder hurts like a motherfucker."

"Joey…"

"I'm not sure what's going on. It's either broken or dislocated, or I don't know what. I think I need to get to a hospital."

"Okay," she said. "How can I help?"

"Can you get here?"

"Yeah, I can come."

"Baby, what's going on?" said Joey. "You sound funny."

"No, it's just… You sound like you're in a lot of pain. I can hear it in your voice."

"I am."

"Did you get a look at the car? The license plate?"

"No, it was too fast. The guy plowed into a trash can just a couple feet away from me, and then swerved away and took off. He kicked up a lot of dust. All I remember is blue."

"Did anybody else see it?"

"No. There was no one else around."

She paused again. "Okay," she said. "I'll get there as soon as I can."

"Wait. Sarah, how are we gonna do this? You don't have a car and neither do I."

"We'll figure something out," she said. "I'll get a ride, and we'll figure something out when I get there."

He hung up the phone. He already felt a little better. He knew he'd feel even better once she arrived.

It happened every time. She'd show up at his apartment and the place would just feel more like a home as soon as he saw her face. He'd feel lighter somehow. It scared him sometimes, but he usually stopped thinking about it once they got into bed and time stood still and the world turned itself inside out in ways he could barely comprehend.

He'd thought about asking her to move in with him. They could be together more often that way, and they'd save money on rent. But he knew she liked time to herself. She liked her own space. He didn't want to ruin a good thing.

But it wasn't just the alone time with her. There were other times too. She'd walk into the room at the warehouse where they rehearsed every week, and he would instantly feel excited and calm at the same time. He thought of all the times when they'd take the stage before a gig, and he'd get jittery just before the set would start. The crowd would be stoked, and the room would practically be vibrating with energy. He'd always feel that last moment of apprehension, like he'd forget the first notes or something. And then he'd look over at her and she'd smile at him, and he'd feel clearer, more centered.

How could he not have fallen for her? Everyone did. She was every band's dream, a magnet that pulled people in every night. It wasn't just the voice. It was the face, the figure, the outfits, the moves, the whole package. She was an alluring paradox of wholesomeness and seduction, all of it completely instinctive and never contrived—a natural outward expression of how she felt the music inside.

The guys in the crowd would stand transfixed in the middle of a song, sometimes in the back of the room, staring at her like she was some kind of apparition. You'd think their girlfriends would be resentful or even furious, but half the time they were reacting the same way. She was someone you couldn't tear your gaze away from.

Sometimes he couldn't believe it. He couldn't fathom how he'd gotten so lucky.

But sometimes he worried too. He knew he wasn't the only guy who'd walk a mile for her at any given moment of any given day. He'd seen the predatory glances from the sketchy club owners. More often than not, they were stares more than glances. He'd stood in countless back alleys, loading and unloading their gear from the van before and after the gigs. Questionable characters would be hanging around in the late hours after last call and the locking of doors. A girl like Sarah couldn't be too safe. He'd even bought her a can of mace, just to have as a precaution. She didn't like it, but she kept it with her.

He'd bought one for himself too. He'd invested a lot of money in his gear, never mind everybody else's stuff that went into and out of the van three or four nights a week. If his ax or his amp ever got boosted, he'd be sleeping under some stairway or out on the streets completely. He figured the extra protection couldn't hurt.

He checked the clock. Twenty minutes had passed since he'd hung up the phone.

"Come on, baby," he whispered. If he could just see her, it would be better.

Ten minutes later, he heard footsteps in the hall. He recognized them immediately.

He looked up at the sound of the key in the lock. Seconds later, Sarah stood framed in the doorway. Her straight brown hair cascaded past the shoulders of a white sleeveless blouse that she'd tied off over her bare midriff. A pair of faded denim shorts hugged her narrow hips, and the two-inch heels of her leather sandals made her long legs appear even longer. Even in his compromised state, Joey felt some part of himself stir, someplace well south of his aching shoulder.

She stepped through the doorway, her face etched with tension, and tossed her purse on a chair. "You okay?"

"Hurts like hell," he said. He looked past her at the door she'd left open. "How'd you get here?"

"I got a ride."

"From who?"

She paused. "Brian."

Joey looked at her in silence for a second or two. "Brian Sutcliffe."

"Yeah."

Joey felt a new wave of tension, one that had nothing to do with his shoulder.

"He's on his way up," said Sarah. "We'll help get you into the car." She tried to sound nonchalant, but something seemed forced.

Joey shook his head. "Sarah, no."

"What's the matter?"

"Really?" he said. "I kind of thought you'd have figured it out by now. I just don't like—" He stopped himself at the sound of footsteps in the hallway just outside the door.

They both turned as a slim figure, just a couple of inches taller than Sarah, stepped through the doorway. He had collar-length light-brown hair and blue eyes. The three or four days' worth of stubble on his tanned face seemed as carefully planned as the number of unfastened buttons down the front of his black shirt.

"Heya, Joey. How's the arm, buddy?" The sincerity sounded condescending, far from genuine. But it didn't matter. The last thing Joey wanted from this guy was sympathy.

Joey looked at him with hard eyes. "Been better."

Joey didn't like this guy. He never did. His mere presence in the apartment felt like a violation.

Brian Sutcliffe was a club owner and a promoter. He owned a chain of three successful music venues around Erie County. He had sufficient pull to bring in up-and-coming acts from all over the country, and many of them had experienced a bump in success as a result of his influence.

He'd been hanging around Water on the Sun for several weeks now, showing up at almost every gig, even showing up at a few rehearsals, gradually insinuating himself into the band's circle. All the while, he'd been talking a good game. Recording contracts, television appearances, and national tours. Joey had been watching the guy for weeks, and what he saw was a series of calculations that had very little to do with the band and everything to do with Brian Sutcliffe.

He saw something else too. Something slick and insidious. He'd been watching the way Sutcliffe looked at Sarah for the last several weeks, and he was certain there was a separate agenda focused on something more primal than the business of music.

"Sarah told me," said Sutcliffe. He shook his head. "That stretch of West Twenty-sixth is kind of a hellhole. Lotta bars. Hell, I wouldn't be surprised if the Ground Round on that same block was selling liquor at this point. People get loaded, day or night, and then get in their cars. It's nuts."

Joey looked back at him but didn't answer. He turned and stepped toward the window overlooking the parking lot behind the apartment building. Outside, the evening light was inching toward twilight, and the streetlamps along the adjacent block were just starting to glow. He looked down at the parking lot, and something hard and ugly immediately took shape in the pit of his stomach.

A Mustang—late model, maybe a seventy-two or seventy-three—parked close to the back door of the building with hazard lights flashing.

He kept his eyes on the car for several seconds. Even in the waning light, there was no mistaking the color.

He turned away from the window and looked at Sarah. She seemed to have trouble meeting his gaze.

The thing in the pit of his stomach grew harder and uglier. And colder.

Sutcliffe glanced at them, his gaze calculating—as always. "Might be an easy fix, Joey. I'm no doctor, but it might just be dislocated."

Joey looked at Sutcliffe without saying a word. He looked toward the window. He looked at Sarah. A razor-sharp silence filled the room.

"Give me a minute," he said finally. "Then we'll go."

He headed into the kitchen and Sutcliffe called to him from the living room. "It's a little chilly out there, buddy. Might want to grab a jacket."

Joey opened a kitchen drawer and rummaged through the random contents. "No point," he answered. "I can't put it on over this shoulder. Buddy."

He kept rummaging until he heard Sarah's voice just a few feet behind him in the kitchen doorway. "Joey? What are you doing?"

He closed the drawer. "Nothing," he said. "Just getting my wallet and my keys."

He turned and looked at her. He felt a hardness in his face that he couldn't control. Judging from her expression, it was fairly evident.

He stuffed his good hand into his pocket and brushed past her. "Let's go," he said. "I need to do something about this."

He felt her eyes on him as he moved into the living room.

Sutcliffe tilted his head toward the door and hallway beyond. "My car's downstairs," he said. "Right by the back door."

"I know," said Joey. "I saw it through the window. Blue Mustang, right?"

Sutcliffe nodded, his eyes turning wary. "Right." He looked at Sarah, then back at Joey. "Let's get you downstairs and into the car. Can you make the stairs?"

He started to reach for Joey's good arm to offer assistance, but Joey sidestepped the gesture. "I got up here myself," he said. "I can make it back down."

They moved silently down the stairs. Sutcliffe took the lead and Joey followed a couple of steps behind. Sarah brought up the rear. Joey used the railing to steady himself, moving slowly and doing his best to minimize the natural swing of his shoulders. Holy Jesus, it hurt.

They reached the bottom and exited the building through the back door, where Sutcliffe gestured toward the car parked no more than twenty feet away. "Sarah, why don't you get in the back?" he said. "Be easier for Joey to get into the front with a bad arm."

Sutcliffe looked at Sarah, but she avoided his gaze by tilting her head away and brushing the hair from her face. She opened the door and climbed into the back seat.

Joey approached the car on the driver's side. From the corner of his eye, he saw the confusion on Sutcliffe's face. "I think you want this side, Joey. You can't drive with a bad wing."

Joey didn't answer. He stole a quick glance at the front of the car as he walked past the grill and made his way around to the other side of the vehicle. He eased himself into the passenger seat in front.

Sutcliffe got in behind the wheel. Seconds later the car was in gear, pulling away from the building and out of the lot.

Joey touched the pocket of his jeans with his good hand and felt the lump inside. The can of mace he'd dug out of his kitchen drawer.

He had just left World of Music earlier in the afternoon when the blue car came up at him fast and nearly took him out. The shop was on a rough stretch of West Twenty-sixth, but the place had been around for nearly twenty years, and they were a reputable operation. They carried a good line of guitars and basses, and they always took care of his gear when he needed adjustments or repairs.

When he called Sarah and asked her to come and help, he hadn't told her anything about where he'd been when it happened. Yet somehow Sutcliffe knew.

And the gash on the front fender of Sutcliffe's car looked fresh. Like maybe he'd scraped a chunk of metal sometime in the recent past. Like maybe a trash can.

And now Sarah, who'd always been so good at putting him at ease, couldn't seem to look him in the eye after she showed up at his apartment with Sutcliffe.

He'd deal with her later. The betrayal stung him hard, but there was no time to think about that now. His first order of business was Sutcliffe.

He'd wait for the right moment.

His first thought was the parking lot outside the hospital once they got to the emergency room until he considered the possibility that Sutcliffe may have had no intention of going there at all.

It was then that the hard, ugly thing in his stomach started to heat up, and he realized that his position might be even more compromised than he'd thought.

He'd have to do it somewhere else. The sooner the better.

Maybe a stoplight. Or a side street with no traffic that could result in a collision.

He'd wait for the right moment.

And then he'd go for the eyes.

Three Mile Smile

(From the album, Night in the Ruts)

Jeffrey Marks

"I hope you have a good excuse," Hank Zimmerman said, staring at the dead body. The local sheriff had been born for this part, his beady eyes watching every move while he held up his chin. Despite the police department's small budget, he wore the paraphernalia of his time in Afghanistan. He loved every reminder of his position in Hudson.

I'd returned from lunch and found a woman dead on the floor of my office. An ambulance, the coroner's van, and a few random cars gave me a hint. She had been young—maybe twenty-five, under thirty—and blond. Two things marred her beauty: the bullet hole in the middle of her forehead and the bright red lipstick smeared on her face.

"I came back and found her. Must have happened while I was eating." My hands were getting twitchy. I hadn't seen a dead body since my time in the service. Zimmerman took it easy on me, as he was one of the few who knew why I hadn't applied for the police department when I'd returned home.

"When exactly was that? Start lunch at nine a.m., right?" Hank said, punctuating it with a snide laugh, making me want to wipe it off his face.

My private investigation business was slow but not dead, especially since I paid alimony by running quick background checks for my ex-wife and her carousel of roommates and tenants. "Eleven-thirty to one," I replied, not wanting to make this worse. I knew he'd check out my alibi to rib me about my hours.

He sighed and then looked at me. "You have no reason to act like you're the most likely suspect. It's clear from the crime scene that she was killed in her car—parked in your lot here—and her body dragged up a flight of stairs. She knew her killer. She was facing him when he shot her. Our chances of pulling prints are slim, and none. The dash of the car is covered with her brains and blood. We're looking for a strong guy or maybe two men. I'm doubting that the shooter was a woman."

My office was on a back street in Hudson, which meant a street no one visited. I doubted that anyone would have heard the shot or seen the body be lugged up the stairs to my office. I never needed security cameras in my daily routine of divorce cases and custody battles.

One tech said, "Weapon looks to be a .40, probably a Glock." It was hardly an intelligent guess since police, military, and gun lovers had one.

"Can I go?" I asked. I recognized the victim and wanted to verify her identity.

He laughed again, this time from the chest. "No, do you know who this is?"

"I haven't had a chance to examine her closely," I replied. I had taken a few photos of her on my phone but hadn't seen her close up. I hadn't trusted my body with the reaction. "But I'm guessing from your response this is Lizette Eichel."

"On the first try," he said. "Now you know why everything must be by the book. I'm going to guess that you don't have any lipstick on you?"

I shook my head. That touch was a mystery to me. Why gussy up a girl with a hole in her head?

I wondered exactly how much Zimmerman knew Lizette's background.

Hudson was a small town with one employer, the Glen Laurel Valley Power Company. Hudson had been around since the 1800s, first populated by the incoming English and Scottish immigrants. Later, during the European wars, the town saw an influx of Germans. The families still took pride in the length of time they'd been here—with the Anglo names feeling they had more right to Hudson.

The Harringtons were a long-time family. They'd held German

names until World War I, and then they'd wanted to appear as part of the community. They had run the energy companies in Hudson, from coal and gas to nuclear power.

Lizette adamantly spoke about the environment, clean energy, solar power, water from the nearby river, and windmills. She'd changed her name to one of the German family names that make her family bristle. She seemed lost in the ever-so-straight-laced family and made every effort to stand out from them.

"Were you expecting her today? Zimmerman asked.

I already had a pat answer for this. Lizette had texted me and told me she had information that would destroy her family. She wasn't in my contacts on my phone, so I couldn't determine whether the text was legit. She hadn't made an appointment. I opted to wait and see if she showed up with a bombshell.

I still didn't know.

"Yeah, the Harringtons come by to see how I'm doing," I responded. I was trying to watch as one of the techs pulled some papers from Lizette's pocket. They seemed far too small to carry the promised information.

Zimmerman nodded and made a note. "Have to ask. Do you know anyone who had it in for her? Any enemies?"

"Besides her entire family, not a soul," I said. "Elections bring out the worst in people." Everyone knew the election was three weeks away.

Zimmerman rolled his eyes. "I don't want to get involved in that mess. It's a one-way trip to zero campaign funds."

The entire town of Hudson knew how elections worked here. The Harringtons provided buckets of money to their preferred candidates—and cups of money to the others. Most of it was funneled through Glen Laurel PAC, making it easier to be "generous" and more challenging to monitor.

However, Dan Payne, running for mayor against a Harrington, refused all campaign funds from Glen Laurel and the Harringtons. To make it worse, Lizette Eichel had been rumored to have joined forces with him, providing him with information that could damage the company—the same information that her text had offered me.

The forensic team packed the rest of their gear, and Zimmerman headed to the door. He closed it with a bang, leaving me to wonder one thing—had Lizette been coming to my office when she was killed—or was she leaving after dropping off her bombshell?

* * *

I decided to get involved. Someone had wanted my skills since they had left her in my office. My first stop was Dan Payne's campaign office. I opted for him because the Harringtons wouldn't object. Only two people were in Payne's office in addition to the secretary and Daniel Payne.

The first was one of the assistant editors at *The Hudson Times*. He likely used all the same rumors I'd heard to get a scoop. The staff at the *Times* had two categories: the lifers who didn't care about the news and those who wanted to make enough of a name for themselves that they could leave town.

The other man was a loan officer at the local bank. Was he a friend or was Payne trying to borrow enough funds to keep his campaign moving?

The secretary sat at the only common-area desk, with the solitary phone and computer. She wore a sweater over a blouse. Both had seen better days. I couldn't see below the waist because she and the desk chair were pushed against the desk. She did manage to have a nameplate on her desk—Dorothea Oakes.

While I hadn't memorized the Harrington family tree, I suspected Dorothea Oakes was a family member. She was an nth cousin removed from the mayor and his brother, the CEO of Glen Laurel Valley Power. Her outfit suggested that her status did not come with its fortune. She was the second member of that family to work for the opposition. I wondered what had caused the split in the family.

When I approached her, her face was about six inches from the monitor. I wondered what was so interesting—maybe Indeed or another employment site. She was going to need it come November.

"Please leave your bag on the chair by my desk," she said.

I recognized that the office had no security. No metal detectors and no security guards. Just this woman and the chair. I had little room to talk since someone had delivered a corpse to my office, but it made me wonder.

Did they know about Lizette's death and the way it was handled?

Payne had signs and buttons, but that seemed to be as far as his campaign went. The two men left with a nod in my direction. The assistant editor made no attempt to interview me, which struck me as odd.

Payne sat in his office, staring at the front door. I walked into his office and waited for him to stand, but he didn't.

"What can I do for you?" he asked. "I don't think I need the services of a private investigator." Even though we'd never met, he knew who I was. That was how Hudson operated.

"Have you heard?" I responded, not sure how to address the situation. My work as an MP hadn't included death notifications.

"I'm lost," he said with a twisted smile.

I sighed and looked straight at him. "Lizette Eichel is dead. The police will be here shortly to ask you some questions."

His face changed to an ashy shade, and for a moment, I thought he'd pass out. However, after a few minutes of deep breathing, he returned to a typical hue. Either he was a damned good actor, or he hadn't known about Lizette.

Before he spoke, I put a twenty-dollar bill on his desk. "In case the police arrive—and they will—we can legally say that I was making a donation. However, I'd like to hear about Lizette's role in your campaign."

He took a minute and said, "Well, she was angry, upset with her family. According to her, she wanted payback."

"Was she more specific?" I asked, looking around and expecting the police. "Payback for what?"

"No, she just said that she knew things, bad things. Never anything specific."

I nodded. "What was Lizette's role here?"

"She did much the same thing Dorothea does," he said, gesturing to his secretary. "She's a member of the Harrington family too. Still, from what I understand, Dorothea wasn't a close relative to the mayor or Lizette."

I doubted the job title. Lizette would have had nowhere to sit and no phone to use. I suspected that they'd worked elsewhere. He was hiding his motive. Was he hiding anything else?

* * *

I thought I'd apply the Fairness Doctrine and give Payne's opponent a chance to talk. Frederick Harrington III had a rally the following day. I wouldn't have the element of surprise because the story of Lizette's death had appeared on the front page of *The Hudson Times*. Still, Harrington likely knew of her death before I'd finished asking Dan Payne questions.

Harrington, the two-term mayor, was campaigning for another four years of allegiance to Glen Laurel. The CEO of Glen Laurel—his brother, Franklin—stood next to him.

Behind them, standing just off the podium, were two security guards. I tried to determine the type of gun and caliber. They simultaneously buttoned their jackets when they noticed me staring.

I arrived late enough to miss most of the speech but just in time for the glad-handing.

"Mr. Harrington," I said with a smile. "How are you?"

"Do I know you?" he asked, looking at me longer than he should have. I knew he'd been informed about the events in my office.

I responded with one word. "Lizette."

The color of his face didn't change, but the expression morphed from pleasant to suspicious. The eyes narrowed, and his lips made a thin line not to give anything away.

"What about her?" he asked. He had stopped glancing from side to side and now focused entirely on me. "Every family has their crazy aunt in the attic," he said, then paused. "Sorry, I didn't mean anything by that." He'd referenced my own PTSD issues, which told me he knew everything about me. "Thank you for your service."

"She was seeing the opposing candidate, and now she's dead."

"If you could pin that on Dan Payne, I'd be forever grateful," he said with a laugh. I wasn't sure how much of a joke that was. "She was sleeping with him. I don't think his wife would appreciate that. Half the town would love to see this pinned on the Harringtons, but I'm not the old-school family. A few of my aunts and uncles would have shot Lizette and a few others to keep the family name clean."

He referred to the few remaining family elders who had ruled this town before the current nuclear facilities. The Harringtons kept them out of sight.

His brother pulled him aside and whispered to him. I wished I could hear, but the general gist would be that he shouldn't talk to me further. I walked away without answers.

* * *

The question that the police had not answered related to when Lizette had been murdered, before or after she'd delivered the information to me. I had not seen the papers in my office, but she wouldn't have left them on my desk for all to see if they were a bombshell. She would have hidden them—somewhere.

Before searching the office, I walked the path from my office to the parking lot and back. The ground was hard, and the stairs to my second-floor office were cement. I found traces of blood, but it didn't help from a crime scene study. Someone had carried her up the stairs before or after she'd visited my office.

Fortunately for me, my office was Spartan. I had a desk, filing cabinets, and a safe that held nothing. The safe was locked; I didn't have the combination here. It was taped to the bottom of an end table at my house. I doubted anyone would have found it because I couldn't remember which end table it was.

The filing cabinets were the logical choice for the papers. Though I had no idea what the information would look like, I rifled the cabinets as quickly as possible. Three days before the election, I thought the voters would need to see Lizette's revelation.

I managed to finish the file cabinets in fifteen minutes. I looked around the room again and noticed something I hadn't seen before. A flash drive had been plugged into one of the USB ports in the back of my laptop.

Black and cheap, it fits in with my décor. I didn't bother with flash drives. I saved all my work on the cloud. I grabbed it and tugged it out of the port. I heard a noise behind me. When I swung around to see, everything went black.

When I awoke, I had two questions: Had the mysterious person taken the flash drive—or destroyed it? Two, why was I still alive?

* * *

The following day was a campaign event, a debate between the two candidates, David and Goliath, in the small town of Hudson. I had a few errands, but I arrived with enough time to talk to the candidates.

I walked around the open-air venue that doubled as the county fairgrounds. This allowed plenty of room for the people of Hudson to stand and listen. Police cars lined one side of the field. I saw Zimmerman's patrol car.

Harrington's team passed out various merch to the crowd, and a few of the attendees wore the T-shirts over their outerwear, trying to keep warm in the brisk wind.

Dorothea was the only one helping Payne. She stopped and started a few times to collect papers. She wrote something on the sign behind the table. I watched as Dan Payne came out and talked to her for a minute.

I was busily looking up something on Google Translate when Zimmerman came up behind me and slapped me on the back. My hands started to tremble again.

"Didn't mean to scare you," Zimmerman said. "I wanted to see if you had any leads, but if you're playing on your phone, then probably not. Do they still have Tetris on those things?"

I looked up from the screen. "I can do better than that. I know who killed Lizette."

Zimmerman started to say something and then shut his mouth.

"I couldn't figure out who was behind the lipstick. I thought it had to be anger or disrespect. I hadn't considered that it might be both—or neither. I started thinking about how it could be an accident or a mistake. If that were the case, I was looking for a woman, not a man, and the field was narrow."

"That was a mistake? She had lipstick up to her nose."

"What if the person applying the lipstick couldn't see well?"

Zimmerman opened his mouth and then closed it again. "Are you saying what I think you're saying?"

"I'm not done. When you scared the shit out of me, I'd been looking up something on Google Translate. Do you know what Eichel means in German? Acorn, and care to guess where acorns come from?"

Zimmerman slapped a hand on his forehead. "Oakes. So, she's related to the Harringtons and Lizette in some way."

"Harrington said something about his crazy aunt—it's a literary reference—but Lizette is too young to fit that character. She's young. Dorothea is much more likely to fit that description. He was thinking of her."

"She can't have killed Lizette. You're saying that this little old woman dragged an adult to your office, killed her, and then drew over the victim's face."

"You're right. The killer is pointing the finger at everyone. Dorothea, Dan, even me—everywhere except the Harringtons. I doubt anyone could plot a murder like this. Plus, Lizette was shot in the car. It would take a cold-blooded killer to shoot someone face-to-face like that. The Harringtons don't get their hands dirty."

"That's it? I'm guilty because I think like a cop and can shoot someone?"

"There's much more," I said. My hands had stopped feeling twitchy as I spelled out the case. "The Glock 22 is a police weapon, though that's not enough by itself. I know you have one, but so do most of the police officers around here. However, the Harringtons knew about my PTSD, which isn't that common. Frederick mentioned it, and I have only told two people in town about it. You're one of them. You two were talking about me. Putting the blame on me and triggering PTSD could make me look guilty."

Payne started to walk away, but one of Harrington's security men stopped him. He was going to listen to the whole situation.

I started putting pieces together. I turned to Zimmerman. "You were in your personal car the day we found the body. Why weren't you in the police car? You love that thing." I decided to keep the flow going, even though it would likely get me beat or shot. My bet was on a physical thumping since more spectators were walking around the fairgrounds now.

Zimmerman started to speak, but Frederick Harrington closed his lips and made a motion as though throwing away the key. So, the sheriff shut his mouth. That was how things worked here.

"You might want to keep those speculations to yourself," said a man approaching our group. "That type of slander can be expensive."

They'd brought in the lawyers as well. Nice touch.

I laughed. "You can't get blood from a turnip." Since everyone was watching me carefully, I reached into my pocket and pulled out the flash drive I'd bought on the way to the debate.

Too bad I hadn't bet on the thumping. I'd have won. Zimmerman practically leaped on me; I didn't think a man his size could do that, but all of him made contact, taking me down. The air burst out of my lungs and mouth, and I couldn't speak as he grabbed the flash drive and stood up. He crunched it under his heel.

"Do you think I only made one copy?" I asked. I hadn't made one, but without a laptop present to verify that claim, Zimmerman had assumed I had made copies. Attacking someone for an unidentified flash drive seemed to add a nail to his coffin.

And I had my answer about the attack. He couldn't kill me because I was one of his suspects. A second murder would have changed the motives and the suspects. Zimmerman wasn't that much of a plotter.

* * *

Nobody was tried for the murder of Lizette Eichel. According to the officers escorting Zimmerman back to the station, he tried to make a run for it, and they shot him—seven times in the back.

Bitch's Brew

(From the album, Rock in a Hard Place)

Mary Dutta

Zoe wafted the steam to herself with both hands, careful not to touch her nose. Her septum piercing was still a little sore. The Sumatra brew smelled like earth and moss, with pleasing, understated notes of payback.

Outside, a slammed door signaled the start of the daily skirmish over porch space between Bitch's Brew and The Briar Patch, bistro tables and flowering plants contesting infinitesimal territorial gains. There was nothing to say about it, even if Zoe had ever deigned to speak to Ashley. She knew the plants weren't long for this world, given that she had been assiduously salting the earth of her enemy for weeks.

Zoe ceded this morning's battle to Ashley and her doomed delphiniums. What were a few inches of splintered porch compared to a feature article in the Chamber of Commerce's newsletter? The interviewer was due any minute, and Zoe had to finish staging the coffeehouse. She cued up some smooth jazz and set out a couple of the board games her soon-to-be ex had left behind. Jason loved games—Sudoku, anagrams, puzzles, party games. Not to mention mind games.

Soon she was plying the young woman from the chamber with a double ristretto and regaling her with an uplifting tale of emerging from a failed relationship to discover her true self as a businesswoman and entrepreneur, laying the female empowerment on as thick as the jam on the scone the interviewer was inhaling. "In a way, my marriage breaking up was the best thing that ever happened to me," Zoe said, pushing a bear claw across the table. "I had to learn everything from scratch, from zoning rules to reading spreadsheets. But that experience made me what I am today." She folded her arms so that her Girl Boss tattoo was clearly visible.

Zoe hoped the free publicity from the article would drive some new business to Bitch's Brew. The spreadsheets she had learned to read had gone from concerning to distressing. If she were in this for the money, she would have cut her losses by now. She took some comfort from the fact that Ashley's business also seemed to be struggling. The day before, a delivery driver had demanded payment in full before unloading her order. If Zoe shared the building with anyone but Ashley, she would sympathize.

Ashley made clear that the feeling was mutual as Zoe entered the city's economic development committee meeting the next night. "Nice nose ring, very classy," she said with a sneer.

"Cute skirt," Zoe said, nostrils flaring. "Still lifting it for your customers?" Ashley tossed her head so hard her butterfly hair clip clattered to the floor. Zoe lifted her foot to stomp it into purple plastic particles but lowered it again. A cat fight would not advance her carefully crafted public image as a successful business owner.

She took a seat in the row ahead of the garden shop owner, scooting her chair back into Ashley's space as far as she could plausibly deny. She chatted animatedly with the people sitting around her, passing out free drink coupons for Bitch's Brew. Zoe crossed her fingers that they would come back as paying customers once they had enjoyed their freebies.

Ashley was too busy fuming to network, the scowl leaving her face only when Jason slipped into the chair next to her. She could at least have the grace to look embarrassed or ashamed. He was still married, at least until he coughed up the financial details that would determine Zoe's divorce settlement. When it came to dividing their community property, Jason put the ass in assets. But then, he had always kept his business dealings close to his vest. Even his company name, JP Industries, left everything to the imagination.

The committee chair's gavel drew Zoe's attention back to the meeting, but her mind soon wandered from the drawn-out discussion of choosing a site for the town's proposed residential/retail expansion. Why was Jason here? Was he propping up Ashley's struggling business with *their* money? Another suspicion for her lawyer to check out at ruinous hourly rates.

The committee's discussion finally petered out. Ashley's hand shot up before the chair finished opening the floor to questions.

"Can we talk about supporting the businesses we already have?" she said. "I'm losing customers because a coffeehouse with an offensive name opened in the same building as my garden shop. I'd like to know how a name like Bitch's Brew even got approved."

Zoe stared straight ahead. No one needed to know how she had wangled that approval, especially not her accountant.

"The Briar Patch is one of the few stores keeping that neighborhood alive," Ashley said. "It's a family-friendly business and the obscenity painted above the shared porch is turning away my customer base."

Zoe snorted so loudly that the chair gaveled for quiet. She had sent her husband to Ashley's business to buy some succulents and he came back with a mistress. What was family friendly about breaking up a marriage?

Ashley did have a point, though. The name offended some people. Painting over a single letter could change the coffeehouse name to Witch's Brew, but Zoe could not afford to also rebrand all the mugs, napkins, and staff T-shirts. Instead, she just kept leaning harder into the hipster vibe, hoping the city's residents would jump on the brash, bohemian bandwagon with her.

In the immediate moment, however, Zoe needed to shut down her rival. "Madam Chair," she said, "my shop's name is not about obscenity. It's about women taking ownership of a term that's meant to be an insult and denying its power to the people who use it against us."

She stared at Jason long enough for people to notice, then continued her speech. By the time she finished, the motley group of protestors who showed up at every meeting, this time to agitate about the threat to the local ecosystem from unbridled development, gave her a standing ovation. Their emotional support dog Che (the subject of last month's protest) danced excitedly and piddled on the floor.

Zoe was not surprised they had her back. When she opened her business, she had made it known that she did not impose an upcharge for plant-based milk, unlike the major coffee chain they had been protesting. They have been loyal customers ever since. What Zoe lost in markup she made up for in positive press and a steady income stream from the dairy-free devotees.

The protestors took their usual seats at Bitch's Brew the next morning, downing lattes and macchiatos to gear up for another day of almond- and oat-fueled activism. Zoe always included a treat for the support dog, who was more interested in lifting a leg to water the multiple flats of dark green plants that suddenly littered the porch than in his pup cup of vegan whipped cream. Ashley had launched a dawn offensive to make incursions into Bitch's Brew territory, in what Zoe could only assume was retaliation for her triumphant council meeting speech.

"Che, no!" a woman with foot-long braids shouted, leaping to her feet, and yanking the dog back from where he nosed the plant leaves.

"What's wrong?" Ashley said, tripping over one of the flats as she stepped onto the porch. She turned a confused gaze from it to the agitated woman.

"English Ivy can be poisonous to dogs," the protestor said, clutching a squirming Che until he yelped. She then treated Ashley to a graphic description of the gastrointestinal issues that could result if a dog ingested the perilous plant.

"And English Ivy is a non-native plant species," a man in a Woody Guthrie T-shirt said, pointing an accusing finger at the offending ground cover. "Invasive species are as big a threat to the local environment as developers. You are destroying biodiversity. Have you no shame?"

The protestors were all on their feet now. They linked arms (freeing

Che, who finished his whipped cream and started eating the cup that had held it), formed a human chain along Ashley's side of the porch, and chanted "Shame! Shame! Shame!"

Zoe left them to it, flashing a smile at Ashley as she went. Her rival gave her a look as poisonous as the ivy. The garden shop owner remained on the porch, attempting to reason with the protestors, whose antics dissuaded more than one potential customer from entering The Briar Patch. They veered instead to Bitch's Brew, settling into the bistro chairs to enjoy the show. Eventually, Ashley trundled away a wheelbarrow full of the offending plants to the cheers of her detractors. The protestors straggled off, as did their audience, leaving Zoe to collect crumpled napkins and logo mugs from the now-deserted porch.

"You did this." A sweaty Ashley, hair straggling from her honey-bee hair clip and dirt streaking her pansy-patterned dress, stood at the foot of the steps. Zoe turned her back and carried her tray of detritus into her café, letting the door slam in her wake. She took no responsibility for the protest. Ashley earned people's enmity all on her own. What did she expect for poisoning puppies?

Things soon returned to normal. The Briar Patch's few customers trickled in and out unimpeded. The protestors sat on the Bitch's Brew side of the porch each morning, casting about for their next cause. But then, one day, they lay down on the steps instead. Zoe, engrossed in trying to make sense of her books before a meeting with her accountant, did not notice until she heard the mooing. She stepped outside to find the activists splayed in dramatic poses, blocking access to Bitch's Brew. Che stood at the center of the tableau, tugging on the tail of his owner's cow costume.

It took a while for Zoe to convince one of them to revert to human speech. "We've been hearing from community members," the man said from his supine position, holding up his phone and scrolling through a lengthy string of notifications. "We can no longer in good conscience patronize a business that helps perpetuate the brutality of the dairy industry by selling milk products." A chorus of moos greeted his statement, along with a single bleat. Zoe duly noted the goat milk objection.

In the parking lot, a group of four women climbed out of a car, surveyed the strange state of affairs, then climbed back in and drove away. Zoe's accountant pulled into the spot they vacated and picked his way up the stairs, stepping over limp limbs and rubber udders.

He pulled Zoe aside. "You should call the police."

"I can't. I need their business. Their protests never last long. They'll move on to the next crusade soon."

The accountant shook his head and went inside.

Every coffee place in town serves dairy milk, Zoe thought. Why are they picking on me? "You did this," she said, looking over at The Briar Patch. Ashley must have posted all those comments targeting Bitch's Brew. She had plenty of free time given how few customers she had. And of course, Jason probably helped her. Speaking of time, Zoe's accountant charged by the hour. She hurried after him.

He looked up as she entered, pushing her spreadsheets to one side.

"You've got a decent offer on the table from the building's new owner to break your lease," he said.

Ah yes, the mysterious Judi Prentiss LLC. Talk about female empowerment. Judi managed to be both a woman and a corporation. But when she bought the building, she inherited the leases, which did not include an early termination clause. Zoe wasn't going anywhere, even though Jason's divorce lawyer thought the buyout would help simplify the settlement.

"This is a terrible location," the accountant continued. "There's no foot traffic. All the other storefronts are empty. Why did you even open your coffeehouse here?"

Because it was the only retail space that put her in front of her husband's mistress every day. And because Jason hadn't wanted her to move into the vacant shop, presumably to spare poor Ashley's feelings.

"Take the money," her accountant said.

"It's not about the money."

"It's very much about the money if you can't pay your bills. Why don't you collaborate with your neighbor. Use some of her plants for herbal tea. Drive business to each other. Just talk to the woman."

"That's not going to happen," Zoe said, and started pulling espresso shots for lattes to tempt the boycotting bovines into reconsidering their stance. The free brews, and the realization that the unsupervised Che was chewing his way through the Briar Patch's bags of organic fertilizer, got them off the steps, into a conversation, and eventually on their way.

The protestors convened on the porch as usual the next morning, assuaged by Zoe's promises to educate herself on the evils of dairy, and to discount their orders for the foreseeable future. She had waited until her accountant left to make that last promise. Better customers paying half price than no customers at all.

The only member of the group who appeared uncomfortable after the previous day's kerfuffle was Che, who suddenly began gagging. "It's the English Ivy," the braid lady shouted, knocking over her chair as she jumped to her feet. "I knew that Briar Patch woman was a liar." But what Che eventually choked out was not leaves but a wad of plastic packaging. Another group member gingerly examined it, squinting at the type. "Weed killer," he said. The protestors gasped, then rushed en masse to examine Ashley's fertilizer stock where Che had partied the day before. "Pesticides," Zoe heard them exclaim. "False advertising. Reckless. Consequences." Music to her ears.

The protestors stormed back toward the porch and started shouting for Ashley. She peered out from behind the locked screen door of her store.

"We'll be back," the Woody Guthrie fan said, shaking his fist, "and you'll be out of business." They thundered off the porch to start wreaking their vengeance.

Ashley emerged as Zoe righted the toppled chair.

"You did this," she said. "You planted those bags of weed killer outside my shop just like you planted those flats of ivy on the porch."

"You're crazy." It was the first thing Zoe had ever said to Ashley.

"You sicced the protestors on me for selling milk."

"I don't know those people. They're out here drinking *your* coffee every morning."

"Well, look at your surveillance videos," Zoe said, waving at the camera tucked into an upper corner of the porch ceiling. "They'll show you I never went near your precious business."

Ashley flushed. "I canceled the contract," she said. "Jason said it wasn't worth paying for."

"And he was obviously wrong about that, like he is about so many things. What else did he tell you?

"That you opened a business next door to me because you thought he would be here all the time. You're obsessed with him, and that's why you're holding up the divorce."

"*He's* holding up the divorce by refusing to provide full financial disclosure. I've spent a fortune on lawyers to chase down JP Industries holdings. Like the beach house in Cabo San Lucas that he's claiming as his primary residence."

"That's ridiculous," Ashley said. "Jason isn't moving to Mexico. He knows I'm trying to save The Briar Patch. Although…"

"Although what?"

"He's encouraging me to take Judi Prentiss's offer to buy out the lease. He must want me to go with him." She smiled smugly.

"He wants me to take the landlord's offer too," Zoe said, "but that doesn't mean he wants me along in Cabo. He thinks if I give up my business, I'll go back to being a clueless doormat and he can screw me over on the divorce settlement."

Ashley shook her head, the butterfly clip dancing side to side. "Jason doesn't play games."

Jason loved games. And he loved keeping secrets. Whoever Ashley was in love with, he bore no relation to the man Zoe knew. Ashley continued talking, but Zoe tuned her out. She was playing a game in her head.

"Judi Prentiss," she said.

Ashley paused in her defense of Jason. "The building owner?"

"It's an anagram," Zoe said. "For JP Industries"

Ashley stared at her. "I don't see—"

"No, you don't." Zoe paced the length of the porch. "Jason owns the building, but he doesn't want either of us to know because he wants us to take a low-ball offer to break our leases. Then he'll turn around and sell it to the developer for a pile of cash."

She whirled around and started back toward Ashley. "Don't you get it? Once the developer acquires this last building, they can raze the entire neighborhood for the residential/retail expansion the city is planning."

Ashley shook her head again. "No. You're just saying that because—"

"For god's sake," Zoe said, "didn't you learn about zoning when you started your business? You sat through a whole meeting about it the other night. I thought Jason was there to support you, but he was there to see how close he was to sealing his deal."

She resisted the urge to shake Ashley until her ladybug hair clips flew off. "Jason is the one who's behind all the attacks. He knows the protestors are here every day, so he kept setting them off. And he had you turn off your security camera so you wouldn't see him putting the plants and fertilizer in front of your shop. He's trying to kill our businesses and get us to leave."

Ashley dragged one of Bitch's Brew's bistro chairs onto her side of the porch and lowered herself into it. "Jason wouldn't do that to me," she said. "He loves me."

"Funny, that's exactly what I said when I found out about you," Zoe said. "But now I'm guessing he only got involved with you to convince you to close The Briar Patch. Hasn't he been trying to do that since the day you sold him those succulents?"

Ashley sat stunned while Zoe continued her march up and down the porch. Then she let out a roar and started hurling flowerpots over the porch railing, followed by a volley of Bitch's Brew mugs. The pile of shards, petals, and dirt grew until she collapsed sobbing back into her chair.

Zoe could not ask for a more utter defeat of her rival, who was well and truly vanquished. She could even sympathize with her. A little.

She pulled a chair next to Ashley. "Truce?"

"Truce," Ashley said, wiping her nose onto the primrose-patterned sleeve of her dress.

"The way I see it," Zoe said, "we have two possible plans of attack. Plan one, we refuse to break the leases, the developer chooses another site, and Jason's plans fail spectacularly."

Ashley sighed. "Both our businesses will probably fail too, then," she said. "I'm about to go under. I don't want to be stuck in The Briar Patch with a bankruptcy."

"And I've accomplished what I started out to do," Zoe said, discreetly not mentioning that it was humiliating Ashley. "I'm done fooling with the Bitch's Brew."

"What's Plan Two?"

"We hold out for ten times the money that Judi Prentiss LLC is offering and use it to make a brand-new start. But that only works if we stick it out together."

"Make it twenty times the money and you've got a deal," Ashley said, holding out a hand covered in snot and potting soil. Zoe hesitated, then took it. What was a little nastiness between friends?

The Reason a Dog

(From the album, Done with Mirrors)

Tom Mead

They're watching the girl on CCTV; a boxy, blocky shape under strip lights white as static. Kay Donnelly has been brought in because she has a daughter about the same age. Now Kay is huddled around the monitor with the others, gripping her coffee mug tight.

"We haven't IDed her yet," Stroud tells her, nodding at the little screen, and the girl sitting so eerily still in interview room 5.

"She looks older than the others," Kay observes. "Sixteen-seventeen I'd say."

Stroud shrugs. "Your guess is as good as mine."

The girl (whose church name is "Leah") looks at her coldly when she steps into interview room 5. There are strands of long blond hair over her face, but bare patches of scalp, as though she has wrenched it away in clumps.

"Hi, Leah. My name is Kay Donnelly. Are you thirsty? Can I get you something to eat or drink?"

"No. Thank you."

"How old are you, Leah?"

"Nineteen."

Kay nods, eyes flicking toward the camera in the corner of the ceiling. "Now, the first thing I want you to know is that we're on the same side, you and me. Okay? All I want is to piece together what happened at Greyridge Farm. Do you think you can help me with that?"

No response. Kay persists: "Can you tell me your name? Your real name, I mean. Not the name Daniel gave you."

"Please," says Leah, closing her eyes, "I don't want to talk about Daniel."

Kay thinks about this. "All right," she says. "Instead, why don't you tell me how you first met Ernie Katz?"

* * *

No one was more surprised than Ernie when the teller hit the silent alarm. It happened quick—he caught it with his elbow—a single jerking, jabbing motion, and the damage was done.

With the butt of the sawn-off, Ernie popped the teller's nose like a cherry tomato. He should have bailed then. The whole operation was fucked from the start. Bill, the driver, was strung-out, barely conscious behind the wheel. And Al, the second stick-up man, was a psycho. The only one with his head screwed on right was Sam, the safecracker. Banks—even small-town banks like this one—were always a gamble. Here, there were just too many variables.

Ernie should have bailed, but he didn't.

"Clock's ticking," he told Sam, who was working the safe.

Al was still whaling on the teller, kicking him in the ribs, stamping him into the ground. The other staff and customers were on their bellies, hands behind their heads. One good thing about having a psycho on board: bystanders do as they're told.

"Al! Leave him. Watch the door."

The teller was bleeding and gurgling; his skull was no longer the same shape. And all to protect other people's money. Ernie would never understand that.

Al skulked toward the door. "All good so far."

It was strange. The silent alarm usually brought the cops within ninety seconds. Often less.

Sam filled four bags: one for each of the gunmen, and two for himself. "Good to go," he said.

"About time," said Al.

They headed for the door, out onto the sidewalk, toward the waiting sedan.

Then, shrieking from nowhere, four police cruisers rolled into position, blocking either end of the street. It had seemed too good to be true; now Ernie saw that it was.

Al emptied both barrels immediately. Cops returned the favor, hitting him in the neck, chest, gut, and face. He dropped. One man down. Sam dived for the back seat. Ernie threw open the passenger-side door. But before he could climb in, Bill hit the accelerator and careered away into the road. The gunshots must have spooked him. He didn't get far, though. A stray bullet exploded the front right tire, sending the sedan screeching off-course.

Ernie didn't hang around. He turned tail as the bullets whistled past him, ducking down an alley that lay parallel to the bank. He ran full pelt, the sack of money strung over his back, till he hit a wire fence. On the other side was a parking lot. He was already out of breath, and the straps of the sack were digging into his chest, squeezing his ribs.

With the sound of running footsteps and sirens behind him, he started to climb. He'd tucked the sawn-off down the side of his pants; it was still fully loaded.

"Freeze, hands behind your head!"

Ernie didn't freeze. He carried on climbing. Shots echoed around him. Then he dived over the fence, into the empty air, landing hard on the hood of a Chevy. It crunched under his weight, and he left an ugly dent. He rolled off and stumbled away toward the far end of the parking lot. That's when he felt the sharp, stabbing pain in his thigh. He looked down and saw blood spurting. He was hit.

On the concrete between parked cars, he dragged himself along. The duffel bag had come open, and he was leaving a trail of bills behind him, as well as the blood. He began trying door handles, praying to God—or whoever—that he might find one unlocked.

* * *

"I found him," says Leah.

"Where?"

"On our land. A dirt trail near the perimeter. He was hurt."

Kay nods. She's thinking about the Smithville bank, which is the last time anyone heard of Ernie Katz. Smithville is some eighty miles from Greyridge Farm; about as far as Ernie could get on a full tank of gas.

"Did he say anything to you?"

Leah shakes her head. "He couldn't speak."

"He was hurt real bad?"

"I fixed him up," says Leah.

"Where was Daniel in all this?"

She looks kind of dreamy now. "He was away. He was working."

"Okay. What did you do?"

"I went through his pockets. I found a driver's license. That's how I knew he was Ernie."

"And then?"

"Hauled him over to one of the barns. Got him in a wheelbarrow and rolled him over there. Stowed him in a hay loft."

"He still wasn't saying anything?"

Again, Leah shakes her head. "He passed out on the way."

Kay is thinking about this. Daniel wasn't around when Ernie Katz showed up. "And did he have anything on him?"

"Like what?"

"Like a weapon. A gun."

"No."

"What about a duffel bag?"

"No."

"Any sign of a car?"

"No."

"All right. And what did you do next?"

Leah is staring back at her, unblinking. "I took care of him."

* * *

Eventually, the pain woke Ernie. He stirred slowly, flat on his back on a hard wooden floor. It took a while for his vision to come into focus. He had vague memories of leaving the car behind and stumbling along a dirt track. Of a sign that said PRIVATE LAND. Of the white-hot agony burning in his leg where the bullet tore through him.

But that was where his memory faltered. Instinctively, he reached for the sawn-off, which had been tucked down the side of his pants. It was no longer there. Then he remembered the money. What the hell happened to the money? He looked around, and the dingy room began to take shape. It was some kind of loft; he could make out the eaves of a roof overhead, and thin shafts of moonlight spearing a small, square, high window. Bales of hay loomed over him in great towers.

That's when he realized he wasn't alone.

"Who's that?" he said. "Who's there?"

The girl wore a white dress patterned with wildflowers. Her long hair caught a sheen of silver moonlight.

When he looked into her eyes, Eddie felt a sudden rush of terror. Something was badly wrong. "Who are you?" he said.

* * *

"Okay. So that's how you found Ernie. Was he hurt bad?"

Leah nods.

"You took him to the barn, and you kept him a secret from Daniel."

Leah nods.

"Did any of the other girls know he was there?"

Leah shakes her head.

"You were in charge of all the girls, is that right? You were the responsible one."

"I did my best to take care of them."

"Did Daniel ever use you? To recruit others?"

Leah is looking down at her bare feet. She can't meet Kay's eye. "It was always me," she says softly. "Before me it was Miriam. But the story was the same. And it always worked. Every single time."

"What story?"

"To get them in the truck."

A pause, and then Kay says, "What was the story?"

Leah looks at Kay and her expression changes. Her voice changes too; it's high and sing-song sounding, as though she's a little kid again. "Do you like puppies? My daddy has a litter of puppies in his truck. It's just around the corner. Wanna see 'em? Come on, don't be shy. They don't bite. They're really cute. If you're good, maybe he'll let you keep one of them."

"And that worked?"

"Everyone loves dogs," says Leah. "A dog has all the friends he could ever want. You know why? He wags his *tail*, not his *tongue*." She looks at Kay. "That's what Daniel used to say."

"And it worked," Kay repeats.

"It got them in the truck," says Leah. "And you know something? There never was a dog."

Pausing the interview, Kay steps out into the corridor. Leah goes back to looking at her feet.

Stroud is waiting in the corridor with fresh coffee. "We found a body in the barn," he says, no pussyfooting.

"Daniel?"

Stroud nods.

"And what about Katz?"

"Still in ICU. Touch and go. But listen, Kay, this could be even worse than we thought."

"What do you mean?"

"There's a patch of land beyond the barn. Apparently, the girls called it the 'Sunshine Field.'"

* * *

Leah remembered well when Miriam went to the Sunshine Field; the night she took Miriam's place at Daniel's right hand. Dinner arrangements at Greyridge Farm were curiously formal, with a long wooden table in the kitchen. Each of the girls had their designated place, and Daniel sat at the head of the table. But he always kept his favorite in the seat to his right. When Leah first arrived, Miriam was the favorite. She was the eldest. She was the one who helped him procure fresh recruits. But she was getting old—even Leah could see it. Old and jaded. Soon she would be turning twenty. What use would she be to Daniel then?

In the days and weeks before her birthday, Miriam grew quiet and morose. Once, Leah came upon her leaning against the back of the barn, staring out at the fields.

"What's the matter, Miriam?"

"It won't be long now."

"Till what?"

"Till the Sunshine Field."

It was one of the last conversations they had. One evening, without query or comment, Leah took her place at Daniel's right hand.

When the dishes were cleared, Leah finally mustered the courage to ask Daniel what had become of Miriam.

"She had to leave us," said Daniel.

"Where did she go?"

"She went to the Sunshine Field."

After that, the Field became a place of fascination and horror. Leah convinced herself she could see shapes in the soil.

Being the new favorite afforded Leah certain privileges. Daniel took her into his confidence in a way that he never had before. She spent more time looking at his eyes, which were greenish brown, and scrutinizing his face. Behind the hefty thatch of black beard, his features were even and ordinary.

"I could have chosen any one of them, you know. But I chose you. You should feel good about that. Do you feel good about that?"

Leah nodded.

"I like you, Leah. You know why? Because you're quiet. You like dogs, don't you Leah? A dog has all the friends he could possibly want. You know why? 'Cause he wags his *tail*, not his *tongue*."

Leah managed to blot the image of the Sunshine Field from her mind for days at a time. Then she could convince herself this *was* paradise. A place of safety and peace.

But one day, something changed.

Whenever another sister came to live with them, she was given a new name. It was a rite of passage, and the way the sister took to her new name was a solid indicator of how well she would fit in with the other girls at Greyridge Farm. As soon as she saw Abigail, Leah had a feeling she would be trouble. Too spirited. But Daniel would not be dissuaded.

To make matters worse, Abigail's arrival coincided with a long, bleak winter, where the bare, dead land froze hard as bone, and Leah took sick for the first time.

Spring came, then summer, and Leah continued to weaken.

Her hair was falling out. She looked thin and scary, with those bags under her eyes. She knew it would soon be her turn in the Sunshine Field. And then, one evening at dinner, she entered the kitchen and saw that Abigail had taken her place at Daniel's right hand. That night, Leah lay in a fetal curl beneath her sackcloth bedclothes, biting through the flesh of her knuckles so the other girls would not hear her sobs.

And the next day, Ernie Katz entered her life.

* * *

Kay steps outside for a cigarette, taking with her the incident report. She stands in the parking lot, reading about the discovery made by Officer Rodney Carter. He found the sedan on its side in a deep roadside trench, with the passenger door propped open and blood all over the driver seat. The trail of blood led Officer Carter along a dirt track away from the road, past the NO TRESPASSING signs. Then, suddenly, the trail stopped.

Locally, this farmer had a reputation. He was eccentric; he hated strangers. No one knew his last name; he simply went by Daniel. Sometimes "Brother Daniel." Ever since Ruby Ridge, you had to be careful with these survivalist types.

Kay drops her cigarette and grinds it out with her heel. She is thinking about Daniel the lonely misfit, and wondering what conspiracy of circumstance turned him into the strange creature he eventually became.

* * *

Leah brought Ernie water and occasionally food. This went on for several days. The pain rolled away from him like the tide. Nobody else came to the hay loft. As long as he kept quiet, it was as if he didn't exist.

He woke shivering one morning, disconcerted to find that not only was the pain gone, but it had taken with it all the feeling. When the girl

(*Leah, her name was Leah*) brought his water that afternoon, he said, "Leah, I need you to get me out of here." But she just smiled and pretended she hadn't heard him.

There were others in the farmhouse across the way. He knew because he heard them chatting, giggling, crying. Seven or eight girls, all wearing strange homemade dresses. Sometimes he looked out and saw them tending the vegetable garden, feeding the livestock, or hanging laundry from a long white rope strung between wooden poles.

And sometimes he saw the man.

If ever the man (*Daniel, his name was Daniel*) came prowling around the barn, Ernie went still and quiet, and waited for him to leave.

Some nights, Leah came to sit with Ernie. They didn't talk much, but they were loaded conversations. One time, she just sat and sobbed.

"What?" Eddie demanded. He was more lucid now; less spaced. "What is it? Tell me."

"It's nothing," she said, hugging her knees. Then, through tears: "Why did you come to the farm?"

"I didn't have much choice."

"Was it me?" she asked. "Did you come here because of me?"

He frowned into her round, white face. What strange thoughts lurked on the other side of those dark eyes? "No," he said. "Least, I don't think so." A silence hung between them, and then he said, "Leah—can you get me out of here? I can't walk on this leg. But if there were two of us, we could make it work. Please, Leah. You're my only chance."

Contemplatively, meditatively, Leah got to her feet and left the barn without another word.

A couple of days later, Ernie was by the window again—taking care not to be seen—when something happened. In a matter of seconds, all the girls went scuttling into the farmhouse. Then Ernie saw what it was: a police cruiser rolled up in a plume of dust.

Daniel came out to meet it. Ernie could not hear his conversation with the two uniformed officers, but he saw the occasional glances in the direction of the barn—of the hay loft.

Ernie watched from a distance, wondering what was going through the crazy-eyed farmer's mind. Eventually, the cops left, and Daniel loped back toward the farmhouse, to rejoin the girls.

Ernie rolled onto his back, wishing his fever-addled brain would work right.

* * *

Kay has lit another cigarette, and now she is thinking again about Officer Carter. About the twist of fate that led him to discover the abandoned sedan. About his visit to Greyridge Farm, and Daniel's conspicuous refusal to let him look around. Inevitable tragedy, like a freight train powering toward a sheer cliff face.

Kay shakes her head and ditches the cigarette half-smoked.

* * *

Leah felt a stab of panic when she saw the cruiser. If they were found—all these girls whom Daniel had saved—then everything would be ruined. Police could never understand a mind such as Daniel's. Just as she, Leah, had kept Ernie Katz a secret from Daniel, so Daniel kept his girls a secret from a cruel, callous world.

But there was something she had been keeping from Ernie too. Like a nesting doll of secrets. And *now* seemed as good a time as any to play that particular hand. When evening came, the food hamper she sneaked up to the hay loft was heavier than usual. Ernie unwrapped it and found the sawn-off shotgun staring back at him.

Then Leah returned to the farmhouse, where the girls were making preparations. She came upon Daniel and Abigail in quiet conference—the sort of conversation that might have been hers before the long, dark winter that accelerated her decline.

Abigail was looking nervous. There were tears in her eyes.

"Go with the others," Daniel was saying. "You have nothing to fear."

Abigail glanced meekly in Leah's direction, then scurried away.

Looking at Leah, Daniel sighed. "What is it?"

"Daniel, there's something I have to tell you."

* * *

Back in interview room 5, Kay reflects that this girl is going to spend the rest of her life in and out of intensive therapy. That the horrors of Greyridge Farm will never truly leave her. The girl she was before Daniel found her is gone now. It is simply a question of salvaging something livable from the ruins.

* * *

Ernie heard the police before he saw them. It was dusk, and the fleet of cruisers rolling toward the farmhouse was an awesome sight. He should have known the cops wouldn't be dissuaded so easily.

He needed to think. But more important, he needed to move.

That's when he heard the creak of the old wooden ladder. It was not Leah's familiar light-footed step. Someone was clambering toward the hay loft.

Ernie looked round and found himself faced with a white-faced, hollow-cheeked, globe-eyed demon. To Ernie, he seemed seven feet tall. Long-limbed and angular, with a glowing oil lamp in one hand, Daniel filled the space like a spider. "You led them here," he said. "You ruined everything."

He advanced with long, loping steps. Ernie whipped his blanket aside to reveal the sawn-off shotgun.

There came the echo of approaching sirens. The flickering glow of blue lights reflected on Daniel's face. He opened his mouth in a dreadful grin, showing brown-gray teeth, crooked as tombstones.

In less than a minute, the barn was swallowed by flame. Before five had passed, the supporting beams collapsed; the roof buckled inward. There was nothing the cops could do but watch and feel the heat on their faces.

Then, cautiously, they approached the farmhouse. The place was silent and empty—at least, that's how it appeared. But when they got to the kitchen, the officers found that this was not the case at all.

Six bodies sat around the long wooden dining table, each dressed in identical homemade dresses, patterned with wildflowers. In the center of the table was a glass punchbowl half-filled with fruit soda. Some of the girls had sleepy little smiles on their faces.

They found Leah wandering in the fields. At first, she seemed to be under the influence of some kind of soporific. Officers approached her very carefully, but she was incapable of harming anyone. She went with them as quietly and obediently as a well-trained pup.

* * *

Kay pauses on her way out the door. "Is there anything I can do for you, Leah?"

"Do you think," asks Leah shyly, "there's any chance I could see Ernie? To thank him?"

"I'll see what I can do."

For the first time since she arrived in that room close to twelve hours ago, Leah smiles. Her heart is brimming with secret joy. All she wants is to see him one more time; to know she has done well, and that she has earned her place at his right hand.

A beard can make such a difference to a man's face. When it's gone, he could be anyone. Calling him "Ernie" will take some getting used to, of course. But she knows what it's like to be called by a name that is not her own.

There is an art to keeping secrets, and it's one Leah has mastered. She has learned from the best. After all, was it not Daniel who taught her the reason a dog has so many friends?

Dude (Looks Like a Lady)

(From the album, Permanent Vacation)
Steve Liskow

"You need to stop stepping on my friggin' laugh lines."

"How can I help it when you keep dropping them? They're all over the floor."

"Why is that a problem? Everyone tells me you do your best acting on your knees."

I pretend I didn't hear anything when I step through the door, but Stacy and Gwynn glare at each other as if we're doing *West Side Story* instead of *The Importance of Being Earnest*.

"Costume parade," I announce. "Ladies, get your bustles on stage."

The women march out to the set. It's tech Sunday, so we have to see what the actors' make-up and costumes look like under the stage lights, set all the sound and light cues, make sure the props work, and practice changing the sets for the three acts. Watching ice cream melt is more exciting, but it's the difference between a successful production and a train wreck.

Chloe the costumer and Lisa the make-up artist sit with clipboards, one on each side of Pete, the director. Doug the lighting designer sits behind them with a headset so he can talk to the lighting technician up in the booth.

"Where's Tom?" Pete asks.

"Whoops, sorry." I scurry back to the dressing room for Tom Strickland, who is fiddling with his elaborate blond wig. He's performed in about forty of our productions and has the chiseled features you'd expect from a leading man. Today, with a ton of rouge and character lines, his face resembles the prow of an ice-breaker, perfect for Lady Bracknell. Emergency is the mother of invention.

The MidTown Masquers presented *Earnest* as their first production twenty-five years and ninety-nine shows ago, and several of the same actors played younger roles the first time around. That seemed like a great promotion idea until Alicia Standish, who was going to play Lady Bracknell, a role on every woman's bucket list, broke her leg.

The casting committee, in a stroke of either brilliance or insanity—it depends on your point of view—suggested Tom, our original Jack Worthing. I didn't see him—I first came in to play Jem in *To Kill a Mockingbird* twelve years later—but I'll bet he was terrific. Now he gives his wig a final tug and walks to the stage, making a conscious effort to walk like Stacy and Gwynn, who don't need a bustle to make it work.

I join the designers while the actors turn slowly, one at a time. Pete turns to Chloe.

"Gwendolen needs a different gown. We don't want a Victorian ingenue in red."

"I've got a light blue one," Chloe says, "but I need to let out the bodice so she can breathe. I can show you tomorrow."

In the eight years since she joined the Masquers, Stacy has become what Tom calls a "ride of passage." Prevailing opinion is that she can recognize every man in the group by his underwear. It's a tribute to her acting that she's selling Gwendolen's innocence so well.

Chloe looks at the stage again. "Under the lights, it's almost the same color as Lady Bracknell's gown too."

Pete nods. "So are their wigs."

"Joel will have a gray one ready for Tom tomorrow," Lisa says. "I'll pick it up during my lunch break."

Tom is short and Stacy is tall. When they turn their backs, their wigs are at the same level so I can hardly tell them apart.

"I love it," Doug says softly. "With the bustle, Tom's got a better ass than Stacy."

"Probably only slightly less mileage too." Chloe's voice is so sweet I don't feel the burn for a second.

The women retreat backstage, and I call the men onstage for their own costume check, then go to the rear entrance, where two of the tech crew chat with a guy I don't recognize. He wears a red T-shirt instead of black like the techies.

"We open Friday," one of our guys says. "Our one-hundredth show. Same as our first one to celebrate."

Stacy has a costume change for Act II, and Tom seems to be helping her remove her first gown behind the flats. The civilian watches them until I move to block his view.

"How many shows you do?" he asks.

"Four a year," I say. "January, April, July, October."

I tell the techies they need to help with the set change. They drop their cigarettes into the sand bucket and go inside. Stacy and Tom disappear into the green room and the visitor turns to me.

"I know one of the girls in your show." He's about two inches taller than me, and heavier, with lines around his eyes. "Gwen?"

Gwynn Abbott joined us in April. Pete saw her in that production and offered her Cecily on the spot. I hope she and Stacy work things out so she comes back again.

The guy looks at a few old flats and a door unit leaning against the wall.

"How's she doing?"

"She's excellent. You're going to come see her, aren't you?"

"I might just do that."

"Awesome. See you then."

I head back inside to the sounds of screw guns and hammering. The techies label the flats so they know what to change between acts. Acts II and III are outside and inside Jack Worthing's Manor House; they'll rotate the flat with the windows, so the curtains hang on the inside and move the stair unit down left a few feet. Those flats are on casters to make it easier. After today's rehearsal, I'll put glow tape on the floor so actors can enter and exit in the dark.

When the Act II set is ready, I go to the green room and cue the actors. I turn to Gwynn.

"A guy who knows you was outside a few minutes ago."

"Who?" She stands and shakes out her hands.

"He didn't say. About my age, but bigger. Dark shaggy hair and a red T-shirt?"

She shrugs and Tom watches her chest. "If it's someone I know from work, I might not recognize him in a T-shirt."

"Really?"

"I'm a paralegal. All the lawyers wear good suits, and the male paras wear cheap ones."

She joins Ruth—Miss Prism—on the bench for Act II. I rejoin Pete and the designers in time to hear Lisa clear her throat.

"Gwynn looks jaundiced, Doug. Can we fix that?"

Doug talks into his headset. "Dimmers nineteen and twenty-three down two points, and twelve up two." The blues dim and the ambers come up a little.

Lisa and Pete both nod and Doug tells the tech to program it into the board. The scene has no light changes, so we look at second-act costumes and watch Gwynn and Stacy work the bread and butter/cake scene with tea and sugar lumps. Food props are a pain in the ass, but we made it through the cucumber sandwiches and tea in Act I with no problems. Lisa lives in terror of someone spilling tea on a period gown.

After six weeks of rehearsal, most plays are no longer funny to the cast and crew, but Gwynn and Stacy use their own friction to make the scene catty as hell. Even Pete laughs.

"What's with the tension?" Doug asks. "Are they making a play for the same guy?"

"Stacy told me she's between lovers right now," I say.

Chloe's voice turns sugary again.

"When Stacy says she's 'between lovers,' you can take that more than one way."

That burns even more than her previous comment. Stacy works at Younger's Pharmacy, and things are getting nuts now that Covid is taking an encore. Maybe that's why she's got such a bug up her ass.

Pete called it right. Under the outside lighting, Stacy's gown is crimson, more Mary Magdalene than Victorian maid. She and Gwynn exit without looking at each other, and the male leads enter to walk the final page of the scene so Doug can sequence the blackout, intermission scene change, and Act III as one long cross-fade.

Seconds after he brings us to blackout, a scream explodes from behind the flats. I drop my clipboard and leap onto the apron, then dash through the stage-right exit. The others are a step behind me.

I find the wall switch and turn on the fluorescents, then force my way through the clustered cast and crew. A woman in a blond wig and a red gown lies face down between the outer door and the green room.

"Stacy…?" A knife handle sticks out of her back, between her shoulders. No, not a knife, a screwdriver.

"No, I'm here."

Stacy stands in the crowd, her face pale under her make-up. Gwynn stands next to her with her hands clamped over her mouth, and I realize the body's not a woman, but Tom in his Lady Bracknell costume. I put my fingers to his neck but can't find a pulse.

"Don't touch anything." I step toward the outer door and dial 911. When I turn back, Pete, Doug, and two techies are keeping everyone else away from the body.

The longest ten minutes of my life end when two uniformed cops follow me through the auditorium. The cast and crew have fallen silent except for Gwynn's quiet sobbing. She sits on the stage-center sofa with Ruth and Chloe trying to comfort her. I lead the cops backstage and they immediately call for back-up.

"God," Stacy gasps. "Who would want to hurt Tom?"

I can think of half a dozen jealous husbands, but none of them are here. The doctor, detectives, and crime scene technicians arrive, and one comes back to the stage a few minutes later.

"Anyone here have the initials 'D.R.'?"

"Me." Doug raises his hand. "Douglas Ritter."

"Then the man was killed with your screwdriver."

Doug's eyes widen. "But I was out front with a bunch of these people."

We all nod. The doctor confirms that Tom is dead, and the detectives start throwing questions at us. I mention the guy in the red T-shirt.

"You remember anything about him, Mr. French?"

"He said he knew Gwynn."

Gwynn shakes her head again. "I don't know anybody like that."

"I told him she was doing great in the show, and he should come see her. He said he might, and that was about it."

I close my eyes and see the guy again. "He was smoking, and he had a Starbuck's cup. Those might be back on the loading deck if you want to check for DNA."

One of the technicians disappears to check. Ruth says she saw a flash of red backstage a few minutes before Gwynn screamed, but didn't think anything of it because both Stacy and Tom were wearing red. A stagehand heard someone in the green room at about the same time, but since everyone was changing costumes or getting props, that didn't help much, either.

"Anyone have a problem with the dead man?" Harper, the lead detective, asks.

"Well," I say carefully, "he was kind of a horndog. But this is theater, and there's a lot of…well…"

The detective notices that no one looks at Stacy.

"Ms. Davenport, have you had a relationship with Mr. Strickland?"

Stacy licks her lips. "Um, we've…been together. But not in a long time. It wasn't serious. It kind of blew over."

"To coin a phrase," Chloe says. Stacy gives her the same look she gives Gwendolen in Act II, and I wonder if Stacy took someone away from her. Chloe's been with the Masquers almost as long as I have, though, so I tell myself I would have known about it.

"When was that?"

"God, I don't remember. Five or six seasons ago? I think it was during *Crimes of the Heart.*"

"Or maybe *Wait Until Dark*?" That's Pete. He directed both those productions.

"Has Mr. Strickland had any other…relationships among the group?"

So much for speaking ill of the dead. Tom has been divorced twice, both times because of flings here that were a little too public. Even though he's fifty, he still looks—looked—at least ten years younger. Everyone in the cast or crew can name someone he's slept with. Except Gwynn, because she's only been here a few months.

"Let's make life simpler," Harper says. "Anyone who's here today?"

We all shake our heads.

Doug hasn't had time to adjust the lighting for Act III, and the outdoor sunlight levels are too high. It's getting hot and I wipe sweat off my forehead. Under their large wigs, Stacy, Gwynn, and Ruth all look like they're melting.

One of the uniformed cops enters from the French doors and crosses to Harper.

"It was in a prop box, stuffed into a duffel bag."

He holds a plastic bag containing a bottle of pills. *The Importance of Being Earnest* has food props, parasols, and the handbag, but Pete hasn't updated it to include meds. We all stand, but Harper waves us down again.

"Who uses the duffel bag?"

"I do," Ruth says softly. "A Gladstone bag. But I've never seen that before. All I put in the bag was a couple of towels to give it some heft and shape."

"There were two bath towels in it too," the cop says. "This was under them."

"Okay," Harper says. "For the sake of argument, let's assume this is a pharmaceutical. And let's pretend the guy you saw outside was here to pick it up without a prescription."

He looks at Gwynn. "The guy said he knows you."

Gwynn swallows before she shakes her head.

"No. I told you before, I don't know him. And I don't know anything about those, either."

"Lady, the guy knew your name. And nobody's ever seen him here before. He was coming for this, but you were onstage and couldn't give it to him."

Gwynn shakes her head and looks almost as helpless as Susy, the blind woman in *Wait Until Dark*, the role Stacy played years ago.

"No," I say. "If Gwynn was supposed to deliver it, she wouldn't have put it in someone else's prop box. She would have put it with her stuff so she could get at it right away."

Harper frowns as if someone has given him the wrong cue line.

"Okay, let's try this. It was in your stuff, but somehow, Strickland found it, and he stuffed it in the duffel bag—"

"Gladstone bag."

"Whatever." Harper looks at everyone while he regains his rhythm. "He figured he could do something with it, blackmail you if nothing else. Or maybe sell it. Maybe he even knew the guy who showed up to meet you."

Stacy played the lead in *Wait Until Dark*, a blind woman who doesn't even know she has a doll with a bellyful of heroin. It feels like déjà vu, all over again. But Harper's scenario has too many ifs and maybes and what-ifs. They're the kinds of ideas that launch a plot but don't resolve it.

Harper doubles down on his argument, which only shows how weak it is. Gwynn shakes her head like she's mirroring me, but a brown line starts below her left eye and slowly crawls down her cheek, her tears smearing her stage make-up. Harper sees it, too, and stops talking. Before long, we're all staring at Gwynn's face oozing toward her collar.

Chloe finally can't take it anymore.

"Gwynn, wipe your face."

"What?"

"Your face. You're smearing your make-up. Don't get it on your gown."

"Oh."

Gwynn looks for a tissue, but there aren't any on the set, which is for a play taking place in Victorian times. Stacy reaches into her sleeve and produces a handkerchief, which she hands over. Gwynn dabs her eyes, then pats her cheeks and looks at the cloth again.

"Oh, yuck." She's about to hand it back to Stacy but looks at it again.

"Um, this isn't lipstick. What is—?"

Stacy snatches the handkerchief back. Before she can put it away, I reach over and grab it. Sure enough, amid the smears of Gwynn's make-up, I see blotches of darker red.

"Stacy," I say. "Stand up."

She looks at me, her eyes wide.

"Now," I say. "Stand up and turn around, slowly."

She's too stunned to argue. She slowly rotates and everyone gets a look at her fabulous butt, now enhanced by the bustle, but that's not what I'm looking for. I kneel and move around so the light hits her from different angles.

A dark shiny spot appears on her bodice and a smaller one above her waist.

"There." I point to them. "Harper, is that blood? Can your techs test it right now?"

Stacy makes a move toward the exit, but her shoes and huge skirt aren't built for speed. She takes only one step before Harper clamps on her wrist.

"Sit again, Ms. Mr. French, where are you going with this?"

I need a few seconds to sort it out, and I've never been great at improv, which is why I stage manage now.

"The guy," I say. "I think I misunderstood him."

"What the hell does *that* mean?"

"Over the last ten years or so, Stacy's done fifteen or twenty shows with us, and she's always been easy to work with. But she's been a lot edgier this time around."

Chloe opens her mouth and I shake my head before she makes another snarky remark.

"She's had a bug up her ass since the first read-through. I thought it was because she's a pharmacist and her job's been crazy the last few months because of Covid, but that's not it. She's been speeding. She'd have access to meds, like the pills you found."

"No effing way." Stacy's voice is weak.

"Yeah, effing way." I force myself to replay the conversation with the guy in the red T-shirt.

"When the guy said he knew someone, I thought he said 'Gwynn,' but she was nowhere in sight. He saw Tom groping you backstage, and he must have talked to you before, so he knew your character name in the play."

Everyone looks at me when I give the punch line.

"He said 'Gwen,' short for Gwendolen."

"We listed everyone on the poster," Pete says. "For the hundredth show. It's on the wall outside the main entrance."

"There you go," I say. "He was looking for you, Stacy, not Gwynn. Tom was with you, and you didn't have the pills on you. You went to get them, but Tom caught you and you had to put them back. By then, your buddy was gone, so you were stuck holding. You knew Tom was on to you, so you moved the pills to Ruth's bag to cover your ass."

"Speaking of asses, you're pulling this out of yours, Sam." Stacy's make-up is vivid blotches on her pale cheeks.

"No, the blood on your gown is from Tom. You had to shut him up, so you grabbed the nearest weapon you could find, a screwdriver. Hell, Tech Sunday, there are half a dozen toolboxes scattered backstage, and Doug's was right there. You and Tom were wearing gowns and wigs that looked alike. If the blood didn't spatter on your gown—which we didn't see because it's red—we might have even thought you were the target and the guy killed Tom by mistake."

It's so quiet I can hear the lighting instruments ticking from the heat. Stacy closes her eyes and tears trickle down her face, smearing her make-up like Gwynn's.

The cops let her change out of the costume, which Chloe seizes instantly before Harper escorts her out of the building in handcuffs. Even though she wears tight jeans, nobody checks out her butt.

Pete sags on the bottom step of the stairs.

"We have to postpone," he says. "We need a new Lady Bracknell and a new Gwendolen. Sam, we might as well close up for tonight."

"Hang up your costumes and stow your props," I say. Half an hour later, I turn off the lights and lock the door behind me.

Gwynn sits on the hood of her car, her short brown hair still flat from the wig cap she wore all day. In a flannel and faded cords, she might have stepped out of a catalog.

"You okay?"

"I've been a lot better. But without you, I'd be a lot worse. Thank you."

"You feel like pizza?" I say, "and maybe a beer?"

"Actually, I feel like a sad woman. But a beer might help."

She shakes her head. "Gwynn and Gwendolen. Pete should have cast us the other way around. Saved some confusion."

"You're younger," I say. "Better for Cecily."

"Ooh." She cocks an eyebrow. "Nice catch."

She slides off her hood and takes my hand.

"What's the saying? Turnabout is foreplay."

"I thought that was fair play."

"Oops. Freudian slip."

Janie's Got a Gun
(From the album, Pump)
Joseph S. Walker

It was a pity, Wynn Grambling thought, that the funeral marking the end of Senator James Emerson's life also inescapably meant the burial of his political fortunes. Otherwise, the turnout would have made the occasion a career highlight. Twenty-seven of Emerson's fellow senators were slated to attend, along with two Supreme Court justices, three dozen members of the House, six governors, four of the top ten political podcasters, and the Vice President. Grambling—Emerson's campaign manager, chief of staff, and friend of three decades—considered ordering a robocall blitz to stir up pressure on the President to show, but ultimately rejected the notion. Part of the job was knowing when *not* to push.

Given the circumstances of Emerson's death, representatives of the NRA would be tastefully absent, though Grambling assumed the floral arrangement they sent would be breathtaking.

The day before the funeral, Grambling worked out of Emerson's home office. It made for a nice effect when he did Zoom interviews with cable news. WYNN GRAMBLING, LIVE FROM EMERSON ESTATE, with a split-screen showing helicopter views of the mansion on its densely wooded hill. On air, he lamented the loss of a "fierce warrior dedicated to restoring America to the traditions that made us the greatest nation in the world." Off air, he bargained for live coverage of the service and negotiated sequencing and time limits for the speakers. Always a delicate balance when politicians and cameras share space.

Across the room from Emerson's desk was a scale model of a railroad trestle, a trophy of the Senator's success at bringing lucrative infrastructure grants and construction contracts to his home state. The real trestle, tens of millions over budget and a year behind schedule, would open next month, shaving five miles off one of the least traveled rail corridors in America. Grambling had already arranged that it would now be named after Emerson. Two days prior, the senator died on the floor underneath the model, bleeding out, as anchors across the country said while solemnly looking into the camera, after inadvertently shooting himself while giving a gun safety lesson to his sixteen-year-old daughter, Janie.

The carpet would be replaced next week. Somebody had put an oval area rug over the deep red stain, but an edge of the bloodied patch was still visible, a long arc of red edging into black. The fifth time his eye drifted to it, Grambling got up and shifted the rug. He was walking around it, making sure the entire stain was now covered when the door opened and Anders Tilton came in.

Grambling started, feeling vaguely that he'd been caught doing something private. "You could knock," he said, walking back across the room and sitting behind Emerson's desk.

As always, Tilton gave the impression of being half a beat out of step with the actual world around him. He looked at the door he'd just come through, as though checking to see if Grambling was addressing someone behind him. "You told me to come here."

"And you could wear a suit, for once in your life." Tilton had on a pair of khaki shorts and a T-shirt so faded the legend was illegible. He was rail thin, with an untidy, mottled beard and blond hair pulled into a baseball-sized bun on top of his head. Grambling frequently dreamed of cutting the hairball off and shoving it down Tilton's throat, but Tilton was too aware of his value to take much open abuse, even from the people who paid him. Still, there were limits. "This is a house of mourning, for God's sake."

"Ain't they all?" Tilton slid into a chair on the opposite side of the desk. "Everybody's mourning something, right?"

"Spare me the hacky-sack philosophy. What have you got?"

Tilton produced a laptop and cell phone from his backpack, setting them on the desk. Both devices were thickly covered with colorful stickers. Grambling had no idea what any of them signified. Boy bands and TV shows, he assumed. Whatever sixteen-year-old girls cared about these days. The largest sticker on the laptop was a cartoon sun, wearing sunglasses and holding a banner reading DON'T LOOK! Was that a joke?

"You sure this is it?" Tilton asked. "She doesn't have another phone? Maybe a tablet?"

Jane Emerson's room, car, and school locker had all been searched within the last twenty-four hours by men who knew how to search. They found no second phone, no diary, no evidence of any secret life of any kind. "I'm sure."

"Then this is weird, man."

Grambling ran his tongue along the inside of his teeth, willing calm and patience. "Weird how?"

"First teenage girl I've run across whose phone isn't crammed full of selfies," Tilton said. "Hardly seems like she used the camera at all, in fact. Or *any* of it. There are no hidden files, no stealthy apps, and no encrypted messages. The usual social media accounts, but very few posts and no videos. She texted with a few friends, all female, mostly stuff about where to meet or who was driving. Nothing emotional. Nothing political. All the files are schoolwork. Hell, as far as I can tell she never even looked at an adult site. Ain't many teenagers these days haven't at least peeked at Pornhub."

Grambling winced. "She's sixteen. Have some sense of decorum. What about the Senator?"

He'd told Tilton that members of a radical group of activists had befriended Janie, intending to manipulate her into producing—or manufacturing—damaging information about her father.

"Not a thing. He's barely mentioned anywhere. Mostly just notes on a calendar when she did campaign appearances and such. I couldn't find any evidence of anybody asking her about him, or her having anything to tell, unless you count emails with her brother about what to get Dad on his last birthday."

"You checked all her sent emails? No unexplained meetings in her calendar?"

"What did I just say? You either trust me to do this, or you don't."

Something held clenched deep inside Grambling released, a little. "Well. Perhaps our intel was wrong."

"That's just based on what you gave me. If I were you, I'd keep looking for another phone." Tilton gestured at the devices on the desk. "What I see here, it feels incomplete. Like somebody pretending to be a real person. Somebody trying not to be seen. You know?"

* * *

It was well past dark that night when the widow Emerson finally came into the office.

Grambling stood, hanging up on a congressional aide trying to get more speaking time for his boss. "Miranda. I'm told you've been resting well."

She wore a plush blue bathrobe, cinched tightly enough to make it unclear what she might have on underneath. She came across the room at a halting pace, not glancing at the spot where her husband died. "Do you know where Bradley is?"

The location of her twenty-three-year-old son was, in fact, something Grambling had been wondering about with increasing frequency as the day went on. Bradley Emerson, currently studying marine biology in Hawaii, had all of James's looks and charm, but none of his interest in politics. He also had a history of being inconveniently direct with reporters.

"I know his flight landed safely this morning," Grambling said. "I know he was on it."

"I assumed you would have someone there to pick him up." Miranda sat. Her speech was slow, with the careful articulation of the practiced drinker. She'd spent much of the day asleep. Grambling knew, to the milligram, what it had taken to get her that rest.

"I did. They missed him. Bradley always hated being managed. Have you had any contact with him?"

"A few texts. He's fine, he'll see me soon. Won't say where he is or what he's doing. A boy should be with his mother at a time like this."

Grambling came around the desk to sit beside her. "He won't miss the funeral, Miranda. He's just being difficult because he hates the cameras, the attention. At the end of the day, he'll remember he's part of the family."

Miranda looked at the windows. "It is the end of the day."

"You know what I mean. I've got people looking. You don't need to worry about this. Everything's under control."

She kept looking at the window. "And Janie?"

"Getting the very best of care. As long as she needs it."

For a moment she was quiet. "What time do you need me tomorrow?"

"It would be convenient if we could leave for the church by nine-thirty."

"All right. Will you come upstairs when you're done here?"

Grambling leaned back in his chair. "Do you think that wise? Now?"

"What an odd question to ask, fifteen years after you found your way into my bed." Miranda stood. "Maybe you just prefer naughty adulteresses to boring old widows."

She had a little trouble with "adulteresses."

"Don't be absurd. I'm just mindful of how things look. We need to show a touch of respect to James before we can be together. Openly, I mean."

"Respect after it's stopped meaning anything. How fitting for you." She touched his cheek briefly, then started for the door. "I'll be upstairs," she said. "Feel free to join me, once you decide what you owe a dead man."

* * *

Grambling made another dozen calls and responded to twice as many texts. A thousand details to be arranged, not just for tomorrow's ceremony but for the days beyond. When to make which announcements, who to call, and procedures to be followed. At last, he put the phone down on the desk and stood, going to the bar James had always kept fully stocked behind his desk.

Scotch and soda, please. Yessir.

A large one.

Yes, sir.

He couldn't put Miranda off much longer. It would look so much better if they waited, but present that idea too bluntly and she would recoil, pull away out of offended pride. And anyway, why *should* he want her any less, with James out of the way? James had probably known all about it, anyway. The neglected wife, the friend who's always around. How could James not know? And wasn't that a kind of permission? Why shouldn't Grambling go to the willing woman upstairs? Why wait?

The office door opened behind him. *She beat me to it.* When he turned, though, Bradley Emerson stood just inside in a wrinkled sport coat, watching Grambling with his head cocked to one side.

"Uncle Wynn," the young man said. Grambling couldn't read the spin he put on the first word.

"Bradley. Glad to see you. I'm sorry for your loss. Your mother was wondering where you were."

Bradley grunted. "Mom has a way of overthinking things. I've been in my room since eleven." Bradley had a suite above the garage, with his own private entrance. "She's asking where I am, it never occurs to her to walk down the hall and knock."

"Well." Grambling gestured at a chair. "You should go to her, but first there are things we should talk about. Drink?"

"A little man to man? Why not?" Bradley sat. "What you're having will be fine."

Grambling brought the glasses to the desk. "Whatever you decide is all right, but I do need to know if you want to speak tomorrow."

"Do I want to speak tomorrow?" Bradley crossed his arms. "I assume my mother will be."

"She will, yes."

"Let her speak for the family, then. Unless my sister wants to say something."

Grambling kept his gaze level. "Unfortunately, Janie will not be attending the services."

"Oh?" Bradley looked over his shoulder at the rug. "Happened in this room, I understand. Were you here, Uncle Wynn?"

"Of course not. It was the middle of the night."

"Right. What would you be doing here in the middle of the night? So, we only have Janie's account." Bradley stood and went to the edge of the rug, staring down at it. "What does she say happened?"

"Her seventeenth birthday is coming up. James was going to give her a handgun, just as he did you. He was showing her how to load and unload it. Janie can't clearly explain what went wrong. She's quite traumatized."

"I imagine so." Bradley came back to the desk and sipped from the drink Grambling had made him, but he didn't sit. "Where's my sister, Uncle Wynn?"

"She's safe."

"That's good. Where is she, while she's being safe?"

Grambling met his eye. "She's in custodial care at St. Luke's. For her own good. It was a deeply stressful experience, son. She needs rest. Therapy." His voice lowered. "Isolation."

"And if I insist on seeing her?"

Grambling clasped his hands on the surface of the desk. "You'd need a court order. Just for the time being. In addition to her fragile mental state, she's a material witness until the accidental death judgment is formalized."

"Convenient, how you helped every judge in the district get elected. And don't I remember you being a major fundraiser for that hospital?"

"This is for the girl's own good. Your mother is in full agreement."

"With you? What a surprise."

"I don't know what you're insinuating."

"Then I'll be clear. I think Janie's under wraps to keep her quiet. You're going to drug her and mess with her mind until she doesn't know which way is up or which memories she can trust. Until her world is just undone. She'll never get out until you're satisfied she won't talk. Or can't."

Grambling had gone very still, his voice cold. "Talk about what?"

"This is the dangerous bit, isn't it? Where you're trying to figure out what I know and how much of it I can prove."

"I think you're way out in front of your skis, and you should stop before you say something you regret."

"Let's see who regrets what. You don't want Janie talking about the fact that our father has been molesting her since she was twelve." Bradley had been leaning forward over the desk, his weight on his fists. Now he fell back into a chair and picked up his glass. "Since just after I left for school."

"That's a disgusting allegation," Grambling said.

"Haven't you heard it before?"

"Certainly not. And I don't believe a word of it."

"Janie didn't come to you? Didn't tell you this?"

"Of course not."

"Of course not. Because if she had, you would have done the right thing. You would have reported it. You would have protected her. Like any decent human being. You certainly wouldn't have used her to get what you wanted."

"And what is it you think I want?"

"In a couple of days, the governor is going to appoint Mom to finish out Dad's term. That'll put her in prime position to run for governor herself in three years. A couple of solid terms there, and she's on a presidential debate stage inside of ten years. And if she happens to marry you in the meantime, you're standing right there with her. The ultimate insider."

"This is a fantasy."

"Sure, it is. Yours. Are you going to pretend you haven't been sleeping with Mom for years?"

"I won't dignify that."

"And it all goes away if the public learns what a sleaze Dad was. So you made sure that wouldn't happen."

"You're delusional." Grambling picked up his phone. "I'm calling security."

"I have proof, Wynn," Bradley said quietly.

Grambling took three deep breaths, then put the phone down. "There isn't any proof."

"Yeah, I saw your pet hacker leaving a little while after I got here. You probably felt safe when Mr. Manbun told you he didn't find anything. Want to know why? How Janie beat you?" Bradley patted the breast of his sport coat. "She wrote me a letter."

"A letter."

"An actual, honest-to-God, handwritten letter, put in an envelope and stamped and stuck in the mail. Probably the only one she's ever written in her life. She must have known you were in her accounts, Uncle Wynn. Didn't want anybody to have an early warning of what she was planning."

"And you have this letter with you?"

"The funny thing is, I almost missed it. I was on my way to the airport and realized I didn't have my wallet. Had to go back, and there was the mailman sticking it in my box."

"Children imagine things, Bradley. Girls imagine things."

Bradley took another drink. "Hell of a letter. She wanted me to know why it happened when I heard the news. She couldn't take it anymore. The fear, the secrecy. Hating somebody she loved. Finally, she decided she had to end it. Had to tell someone."

"Miranda."

"No. She thought Mom already knew. I'm not convinced of that, but I'll find out soon enough. And Dad never paid any attention to Mom anyway." Bradley rolled the glass between his palms. "But he listened to you, Uncle Wynn. He did everything you ever told him to do. She thought you would make him stop."

"This never happened."

"You told her that nobody would ever believe her. You told her everyone would think she was sick. You told her there's no justice in the world but what we make ourselves. I can give you exact quotes if you want. I've got the letter memorized, read it over and over and over on the flight."

Grambling stood up. "I don't want to hear any more of these sick lies."

"Dad always kept his guns in a safe. That safe, behind you. How did Janie get her hands on one?"

"I told you. It was going to be her birthday present."

"You don't know Emerson traditions as well as you ought to, Wynn. Boys get their first gun on their seventeenth birthday, but girls that age are regarded as flighty. Girls get guns when they turn twenty-one." Bradley wasn't looking at Grambling. He was looking at the surface of the desk. "Janie's letter says she got the combination to the safe from a note on a piece of scrap paper you dropped. Wasn't that lucky?"

Grambling didn't answer. His breath was shallow, his face pale.

"She wrote it right afterward. Said she didn't know for sure what she was going to do once she got a gun. Kill him. Kill herself. Maybe both." Now Bradley did look at Grambling. "I'm betting you were hoping for that. Bury the whole mess and get Mom a ton of sympathy votes for years to come. Janie let you down there, only pulled the trigger once. But you figured you could still keep her under your thumb."

Grambling sat, pressing his palms hard into his thighs to stop them from shaking. "Your sister is a very troubled girl, Bradley. This letter is all delusional ramblings, but it could do a lot of harm and sully a good man's memory. You need to give it to me. I'll make sure she's well taken care of."

"Janie was sure right about one thing." Bradley put his hand in the pocket of his sport coat and pulled out a small, flat automatic. "You don't really know what you're going to do with one of these until you've got it in your hand."

"You planning to shoot me?" Grambling put steel in his voice. "You think that makes you the hero of the story? You were awfully quick to say this started after you left for school. Think that lets you off the hook, boy? Think that doesn't mean you overlooked a hundred warning signs? Ignored how quiet she got? So, who let who down?"

Bradley held the gun out at arm's length, pointed directly at the center of Grambling's face, and pulled the trigger. The dry, sharp click of the empty weapon came at the same moment as Grambling's strangled cry, as he lurched backward, holding out his hands as if to ward off a blow.

"That's too good for you," Bradley said. He dropped the gun back into his pocket, then sniffed and wrinkled his nose. "I hope you've got a change of pants here, Wynn."

Wynn sagged sideways in the chair. "Goddamn you," he hissed.

Bradley stood up. "I'll leave you to work, Wynn. I think you've still got a busy night ahead. An hour ago, I posted Janie's letter to Dad's website. I imagine the big papers have it by now. You're about to start getting a lot of cancellations for tomorrow. You can probably deal with some of them before the police come for you."

"You're bluffing. You wouldn't shame her like that."

"She's not the one who should be ashamed, is she? Janie's a survivor, you son of a bitch. I'm going to find her and help her remember that. She's going to tell her story, and people are going to believe her. As for you?" Bradley nodded toward the safe. "You still know the combination, right?"

Livin' on the Edge
(From the album, Get a Grip)
Adam Meyer

Liv stepped out on the roof, inhaling the ocean smell, briny and wet with a hint of winter chill. The odor was always stronger on top of Perry's twelve-story apartment building than down on Beach 98th Street. She had forgotten that, despite all the hours she'd spent up here over the years.

"Liv!" Perry cried, calling her name from across the rooftop.

He must've heard the door swing shut. She couldn't even see him yet, not with the big metal HVAC units between her and the roof's edge.

"It's freezing out here," she said, making her way toward him.

Moving around the last of the big steel boxes, she finally spotted him. Legs propped on the roof's concrete ledge, a cigarette stuck between his lips. He wore faded jeans, a short-sleeved shirt, and ripped-up sneakers, the same uniform all year long. She zipped up her quilted jacket.

"It's really you," he said, taking a long drag. "I thought you might be dead or something."

"We just texted back and forth last week."

"And before that?"

"Just busy with work, that's all."

"Right, you're a bigshot accountant now."

Not a big shot at all. She worked for a small insurance agency in Far Rockaway, a short ride on the A train. At least she had a salary big enough to move out of the bungalow she'd grown up in, unlike most of their old high school classmates, who, in their mid-twenties, still lived at home. Like Perry, who'd grown up on the sixth floor of this building.

"How's business?" she asked. "Still selling pills to high school kids?"

"Ouch." Perry put a hand on his heart as if he'd been wounded, but he seemed amused. "Of course, I probably got more customers in Arverne than I do on the school bus. And I never try to sell people anything they don't want."

Arverne East was where much of the new development in Rockaway had gone in, mostly condos owned by twenty-somethings priced out of Park Slope. She wondered what the newcomers thought of Perry. Probably they liked him. He could be charming when he wanted, and even when his words were cutting, he hid the sharp edges.

"You remember that summer we were fifteen?" Perry pitched his cigarette away and swung his legs from the roof's ledge, leaning back a little. Liv's stomach lurched, even though she'd seen him do this a thousand times. "We came up here like every day."

"Yeah, I think I've still got the sunburn to prove it."

She looked out over the edge of the roof. From here she had a clear view of the beach, empty except for an old man with a metal detector. Beyond that was the Atlantic, the choppy waves silver and white, gnashing at the shore.

"You look good, you know," Perry said, studying her as he lit another cigarette.

"Thanks."

"How's your new boyfriend?"

"Not so new. We've been together eight months." She sat next to him on the ledge, her back to the view. "You got another cigarette?"

He lit one off his and passed it over. "I thought you quit. I mean, what's your boyfriend going to say if he finds out you've been smoking?"

He'd flip, she thought, and want to know if she'd been hanging out with Perry again. But Mike wouldn't be home for a couple of hours, plenty of time for her to scrub herself clean.

"It's none of his business," Liv said. "Yours, either."

Perry turned to face the ocean and blew out smoke. "The world's gone to shit, you know that? All these rich assholes coming here to

Rockaway, the ones we grew up with moving out or dying off. And all these new businesses coming in too, only I can't afford them and I'm not sure who can, except for these trust-fund kids living off their parents' credit cards."

"None of this is news, Perry. And you can't just sit around thinking about it."

"Don't you see? I got to." Perry looked at her, his eyes surprisingly clear behind his gauzy stoner look. "It's different for you, because you can still get out."

"Come on, so could you."

"Okay, then…maybe I don't want to."

He sat on the ledge, leaning back again. This time she wasn't afraid of him falling but felt panic all the same. What if he was telling the truth? And if he couldn't get out, what did that say about her? Like Perry, she had been born at Peninsula Hospital, twenty blocks from here, and lived all her life on this same seven-mile-long peninsula.

She took a quick pull on her cigarette, the nicotine hitting all her pleasure centers. "Look, did you bring me here just to tell me everything's gone to shit?"

He leaned in closer now. "Okay, I'm going to tell you a story. You heard about what happened to Gene Pizzolatto, right?"

Of course, she had. It was big news, everyone shocked and horrified. Gene was a few years older than her and Perry, a neighborhood fixture. He worked at Pizzolatto's, a pizza joint owned by his father. Gene was mentally challenged, slow to understand things but sweet, and had a big smile every time he saw Liv come in to order a pie.

Gene had a habit of walking alone late at night, at least until one Friday night when he'd been found in an alley off Beach 93rd Street, bruises all over his body. Two weeks later he was still in intensive care.

"Yeah, I heard about Gene. So awful. Lucky they caught the guy who did it."

The details of the arrest were more vague in Liv's mind than the attack. Some homeless guy off his meds had accused Gene of rummaging through his shopping cart and went after him.

"I don't think so," Perry said.

Liv gave him a look. "Don't think what?"

"Gene didn't do it. He's the fall guy."

Liv forced herself not to sigh. Perry had always loved conspiracies. In ninth grade, he'd done a paper about how the moon landing was fake. Liv still remembered how proud he was of the B- he'd gotten—a good grade for him—and the teacher's comments: *Even though this paper is not grounded in fact, your argument is compelling.*

"So…" Perry slid off the ledge. The giant HVAC units had started humming, the noise nearly drowning out what he said next. "I was actually out there the night he got beat up."

Liv felt a faint sense of panic, though she wasn't sure why. "What're you talking about?"

"I'd gone to Milani's, had a few beers, left about eleven, eleven-thirty. Figured I'd take a shortcut over to Beach Boulevard, and when I looked up, I saw them."

"Saw who?"

"I don't know, the kind of guys who've moved into the neighborhood the last couple years—financial bros, only they looked a little rough. Rumpled shirts and jackets, ties pulled off, hair messed up, and not on purpose." Perry looked right at Liv. "One of them had blood on his shoes. Another's hands were all swollen up. The third guy had scratch marks on his neck."

Liv said nothing, feeling nauseous. Probably the cigarette. She pitched it away.

"You know any of them?" she asked. Some part of her seemed to know what Perry was going to say, even before he said it. Just like old times.

"I dunno, it was dark…but one looked a lot like your boyfriend. It's Mike, right?"

Perry knew it was, so she didn't bother to confirm. Besides, he had said it himself, it was dark, and he couldn't be sure. But Liv thought about how she'd gone to Mike's place the night after the attack and noticed the red marks on his neck. He'd told her it was from a pickup basketball game after work, but he looked away as he said it.

"I still don't see what this has to do with me. Or Gene Pizzolatto."

"Here's the thing, Liv. That alley where I saw those guys was only a couple blocks from where Gene got hurt, and the timing would've been about right."

"Except that the guy who beat the crap out of Gene is in jail."

Perry looked sideways at her, as if to say she was being naive. Maybe she was. Perry's worldview was skewed, but sometimes he saw things others missed.

"Okay, if you think those financial bros attacked Gene Pizzolatto, then you should go to the cops."

Perry nodded, blowing out smoke. "Maybe. But cops and I don't really mix. Besides, they like to keep things simple. They've got their suspect and that's that."

Liv was craving another cigarette, only if she took one, she wouldn't be able to hide the shake in her hand. "Look, I don't know what you think you saw that night, but Mike wouldn't do something like that. That's not who he is. He's a good man. Smart and reliable. Decent."

Not to mention he had a degree from Cornell and had grown up in East Hampton, the kind of Long Island beach town where old men didn't piss under the boardwalk and kids didn't dig up broken beer bottles while making sandcastles. His world was a long way from theirs.

Perry shrugged. "If you say so."

"I do. Now what do you want from me?"

"That's up to you, Liv."

"Bullshit. 'Cause if I don't do what you want, you'll judge me for it. But you've been judging me for years, anyway."

Liv didn't try to tamp down her anger the way she usually did with Perry. He needed to know how she felt and that if he kept pushing this, their friendship—nurtured since first grade—was going to be compromised. Or worse.

"You want to know what I think?" he asked, sounding more resigned than angry. "I think that out of our whole class from Beach Channel High School, you're the one who could've gone the farthest. You had the biggest brain and the best grades, and you saw the world in a way no one else did. But somehow you got stuck here…and maybe that's my fault, because you didn't want to leave me behind, and I feel a little bad about that, okay? But not bad enough to tell you to get the hell out of here."

He sounded out of breath when he finished. That might've been the longest speech he'd ever given.

"Well, maybe that's the whole thing in a nutshell, Perry." She stood from the ledge, looking down at him. "You can see that I'm into Mike and he's into me, and even though you don't want to be with me, you don't want me to be with anyone else, especially someone who might take me far away from here."

"That's not true. I'm looking out for you. Because you can do better."

"Bullshit. You've always put me on a pedestal, Perry. Thing is, when someone's up there like that, it's only a matter of time before they get knocked down. And that's what you're trying to do to me."

"Liv, it's not—"

"Leave me alone."

She pulled away, stomped across the rooftop, the wind kicking up. When she turned back to Perry, her hair whipped into her face, strands of it in her mouth.

"You're an asshole, you know that?" She was shrieking now but didn't care. Twelve stories up, no one could hear her besides Perry anyway. "I've let you try to drag me down for years but not anymore. So, fuck off!"

She stomped past the hulking HVAC units. She flung open the door and leaned against the brick wall of the stairwell, touching her neck at the same place where Mike had had those red marks. The overhead light had gone out and she could hardly see.

She waited for Perry to come after her. But he didn't.

Taking a deep breath, she made her way to the lobby, footfalls echoing all the way down.

* * *

Instead of going home to the cramped apartment she shared with two roommates, Liv went to Mike's place.

He wasn't home yet, so she used her key to let herself in. She took a long shower under the three-way jets, steam filling her nostrils. The water was healing. Being here, she felt a million miles away from that rooftop, and Perry, and all that had happened between them.

After the shower, Liv rubbed herself dry with one of Perry's Egyptian cotton towels. It was funny. Her whole life, she'd used Kmart towels and never minded, but now they felt like sandpaper. Every time she used one, they grated, and not just on her skin.

About fifteen minutes later, the front door opened, and Mike came in, shrugging off his overcoat. "Here you are," he said, coming over to kiss her. "I've been trying to reach you."

She picked her cell phone up off the coffee table. "I ran out of juice. And I was feeling too lazy to plug it in. Something going on?"

"No, just checking in."

He disappeared into the kitchen. She heard the fridge opening and then a bottle being opened. "You want a beer?"

"No, thanks."

When he came back, he took a long sip. She studied him. Short dark hair gelled into perfect disarray, high cheekbones, dark eyes that seemed to look right into her soul. The scratch marks on his neck were now faint pink lines.

"You come straight from work?" he asked, watching her get up from the couch. He started to take another sip from the bottle, but she took it for herself. The cool beer soothed her throat.

"No, I made a stop on the way here. I went to see Perry."

He reclaimed his beer, took a long drink. She started to touch his arm and then stopped herself, same as she had with Perry earlier.

"It's not what you think," she said. "He wanted to tell me

something…about you."

Mike looked away, his eyes unreadable. "He gave you that story, didn't he? How he thinks we beat up that poor guy from the pizza shop?"

Liv looked at him in disbelief. "He came to you first?"

"Yeah, a few days ago. He told me what he saw, said that if I didn't tell you everything, he'd tell you himself."

Liv felt her throat close, and forced the words out anyway. "What did you say?"

"What do you think? That he's crazy. Yeah, me and my buddies were a bit roughed up, but that's because we got in a bar fight. One of my pals was talking to this girl, and her sort-of boyfriend got mad, and next thing you know… Anyway, we were drunk, and it got ugly. Look, I should've been honest in the first place, but I just…I didn't want you to think I was some kind of jerk. Because I'm not."

"I know."

"Anyway, I told Perry what happened." Mike started to take another pull of his beer, but it was already empty. "And I told him to fuck off and leave you out of this. As usual, he didn't listen. You don't believe him, do you?"

Liv put her arms around Mike and lay her head on his chest. "Of course not."

"Because I wouldn't…what kind of a person…"

He pulled away and went into the kitchen, got himself another beer. He didn't ask if she wanted one this time.

"You think he'll go to the cops?" Mike asked, studying his bottle.

"No. There's no way."

"I'm sure you're right, the last thing he wants is to get near the police. What about blackmail, then?"

Liv shook her head. "It's not his style. Besides, he doesn't care about money, not really."

Mike looked at her, eyes narrowing. "It's you. He thought it was a way to win you back."

"Maybe."

Mike set his beer down on the coffee table and put his arms around her. "Do you still want to be with him?"

Liv turned her face up to his. "What do you think?"

"I want us to be together. Me and you. Now and in the future." He kissed her, his lips lingering for a moment, mouth tasting of beer. "I'm going to jump in the shower. You want to join me?"

"No, thanks. I just had one." She ran a finger along his cheek, tracing it down to his neck. "But maybe we could get to bed early."

"Sounds perfect."

She stood there, waiting until she heard the water turning on, and picked up her phone. She didn't turn it on because she knew what would be waiting. Messages from her friends, telling her about what had happened to Perry. But she already knew.

After she'd left him on the roof, she had started to head away but she only got about halfway up the block when she stopped and felt a tickle of anger.

No matter what he said, Perry would never let her go. If it wasn't this story about Mike, it would be something else. Anything to tie her to this place. To him. Perry wanted her to be stuck, just like he was.

That was why she turned around and went back up to the roof.

The HVAC units were going loudly, and Perry didn't hear her as she came toward him. He stood on the concrete edge, looking out toward the water. He looked so peaceful. For a moment Liv didn't think she could do it, but then she raised her hands and reached out. As she braced her fingers against his back, Perry turned and saw her, the look on his face more disappointment than surprise, as if he'd always known this was coming.

She had covered her ears against his screams and shivered against the cold.

Now she stopped at the bathroom door, pausing long enough to hear Mike singing. It sounded like some old rock song, the kind her mother used to play on old CDs when Liv was a kid. She kept going into the bedroom, running her hand along the silk sheets, and headed for Mike's nightstand.

She glanced at the doorway again, then pulled out a small felt box from the top drawer. She'd found it here a couple of weeks ago, after Mike told her he wanted to make plans to go to a bed and breakfast in the Catskills. She had thought a proposal might be in the offing, and sure enough, it was.

She opened the box and studied the ring in its velvet bed.

Not just a ring. The most beautiful ring she had ever seen.

She set it on her palm. The diamonds around the edges glinted so brightly they almost hurt her eyes. The one in the middle was as big as a walnut. She couldn't believe he had bought it for her.

When she and Mike had met at one of those fancy new bars over by the beach, the kind of placed Perry hated, she'd thought it was just a fling. How could it ever last, him working on Wall Street, her a local who'd hardly left Rockaway? But he always said that she had more going on than she showed, which she thought was a compliment even though it stung a little. She had passed one test after another, meeting his coworkers, his friends, his family, and when he gave her a key to his place she started to think: maybe he wants this to go the distance.

And she'd clearly been right.

Except Perry and his ravings had threatened to undo everything. He was a part of Liv's past that she'd spent a long time trying to forget, and his accusations against Mike were a direct assault on her future. Did she really believe what Perry had said about Mike and his friends attacking Gene Pizzolatto? For a moment, maybe.

Then she realized it didn't matter.

Perry would never go to the cops, but he'd keep pushing his story. Spreading rumors. Asking questions. Forcing her to make a choice, him or Mike.

That one was easy.

She slipped the ring on her index finger. There was some resistance at first and then it slid right down.

She studied her hand.

Ten years from now, where would she be without Mike? Married to one of the guys she'd gone to high school with, who now worked at the post office or the fire department? Living in a house just like the bungalow she'd grown up in? Waiting for discounts at Shop Rite to stock up on spaghetti sauce and paper towels like her mother?

With Mike, it was different. Once they married, she knew it would only be a short time before they started looking at houses out on Long Island, the kind with big yards for swing sets and weekend barbeques with neighbors.

From outside, she heard the faint sound of sirens.

Liv held her hand up to the light. She studied the diamonds, the way they glittered, and looked out the window toward the dark ocean, thinking about Perry.

She hadn't wanted to hurt him, but he'd forced her. Minutes after she pushed him, she panicked, wondering if someone had seen her slip out of the apartment building. The police would come around soon and might be suspicious of her once she admitted to seeing him on the roof earlier that night. All her careful planning would unravel.

But no, Perry was probably right. The police liked to keep things simple. And Perry's death would look like a suicide.

After all, he'd lived his whole life on the edge.

It was only a matter of time before he went over.

Hole in my Soul

(from the album, Nine Lives)

John M. Floyd

I was strolling down the sidewalk on the one-way street from my apartment to the shopping center and thinking about Annabelle (nothing new, there) when I heard the roar of the garbage truck behind me. They always go too fast, everyone knows that, and I would've probably paid it no mind if the little deaf child from the house next door hadn't sprinted past me and into the street, chasing his soccer ball. I turned to look, and saw the giant truck was headed right for him.

I froze for a second, then shouted to him—in a corner of my mind I heard the screech as the driver realized what was happening and stood on his brakes. The boy of course heard none of this, neither my shout nor the noise from the truck. I broke into a run, and seconds later I was there, in the street and shoving him out of the way. Which of course put me *in* the way. And it was too late to move.

The smoking tires slowed the truck, but not enough. The front bumper knocked me flat, and the truck kept rolling another ten feet before it stopped. When I crawled out from underneath it, feeling a little like Indiana Jones, I found that the only damage to me was a bruised hip and a dirty smudge on the arm of my blue shirt. The boy, sprawled at the roadside but safe, stared at me with wide eyes while half a dozen people appeared from nowhere, shaking my hand and slapping me on the back. The driver, when he climbed down from his perch, was trembling. His face was pale as a stick of chalk. He stumbled over to me with tears in his eyes, pulled me into a bear hug, and then sagged to a sitting position on the sidewalk.

I patted his broad shoulder, nodded to the growing crowd, and assured everyone that I was okay. After checking my watch, I continued on my way. I didn't look back, but I could hear them all talking and could imagine them standing there gaping at me in wonder. I was still a little shocked myself.

I didn't let it slow me down. In the practical part of my weary brain, I saw that the skies had darkened since I left home, with occasional rumbles of thunder, and even though there was no sign of rain, the storm was now crashing and flashing above me like artillery fire. What an afternoon—and how appropriate to my mood, I thought. I felt as if Annabelle had drilled a hole in my soul. Corny, yes, but that's the way I felt.

At one point a sizzling bolt of lightning hit an oak tree within fifty yards of me, blasting it to splinters. The thunderclap shook the ground, and the wind blew my baseball cap off. I trudged steadily on, not bothering to chase it. All around me folks were running inside and sheltering in their homes and peering out through their windows. I paid them no attention.

Three blocks and ten minutes later, when the worst of the fast-moving storm had moved east, a skinny bearded man in a hooded jacket leaped from an alley and onto the sidewalk a dozen feet in front of me, a cigarette in his mouth and a long knife in his hand. "Gimme your money, dude," he said, above the steady roll of thunder. "And stay right there."

I kept walking. When I'd traveled the six or seven steps between us, I stopped and stood there, facing him. I wondered if I should tell him I didn't have any money. Or a phone. Or a credit card. Or even a car to drive to the store. I decided not to, and since he didn't do anything but stare back at me, I raised my right hand, pointed it at his face, and said, "Get out of my way."

Still, he did nothing and said nothing, so I made a fist and hit him square in the mouth. I'm not a big guy, but I'm strong and I'm fast—my punch flattened his cigarette and his already-ugly nose and probably loosened a few teeth. He let out a heavy OOOF, sort of the way those female tennis stars grunt after a hard shot, then fell backward on the sidewalk like a chopped tree and lay there spreadeagled and motionless.

Before I knew it, an older lady with a wooden walking-cane appeared out of nowhere. "I know you," she said, squinting at me. "You're Billy Longwood. You used to date that little redhead, what was her name?—Annabelle? Her grandmother was a friend of mine." Since that was apparently an observation instead of a question, she didn't wait for a reply. She just looked down at the unconscious guy and scowled. "I know this greasy bastard too. He robbed me last week. Took my purse with fifty dollars in it." As if to help end that statement, she drew back her foot and kicked him a good one in the side.

She looked as if she might be considering another kick, so I distracted her by fetching the dropped knife and tossing it deep into a weedy ditch. In the process of doing that, I saw a bulge in the guy's jacket pocket, and bent over to check it. Sure enough, it was a fat wad of cash, mostly twenties and tens and probably freshly stolen. I handed it to the old lady. She grinned at me, stuffed it into her purse, and gave me a fierce hug.

I watched her walk away, counting her money, and then I stepped over the skinny guy and kept going. My wristwatch—the one Annabelle had given me, so long ago—said the store would close in an hour.

I arrived there at four-thirty. I made my way to the sporting goods department at the back of the building and asked the bored guy behind the counter to show me three or four items. He asked my name, and when I told him he introduced himself as "Eddie," a fact that was confirmed by his yellow plastic nametag. He lined the merchandise up on the glass countertop for my inspection and had left to do something else when I heard heavy footsteps approaching. I also heard someone further down the counter let out a surprised gasp.

"Everybody freeze," a gravelly voice behind me said. "I got five pounds a dynamite strapped under my shirt."

I turned to look. The voice belonged to a big, bearded, slack-jawed man in jeans and hiking boots and a baggy plaid shirt. He looked like the world's dumbest lumberjack. In one of his hands was a device that looked a TV remote and in the other was an automatic pistol. An oversized and unzipped duffel bag hung from one shoulder. He unslung the empty bag with his gun hand, tossed it to the worker who'd been helping me—Eddie—and told him to fill it with as many weapons and as many clips of ammo as he could. He added, "Or I'll blow us all up."

I let out a sigh. Would this day never end?

As the new arrival watched Eddie hurry off on his errand, I picked the revolver I'd been examining up off the countertop, turned, marched over to stand in front of the bomber, and pushed the muzzle of the gun up under his chin so hard he rose up onto his tiptoes. His bloodshot eyes went wider than those of the deaf kid's.

"Drop the detonator," I said.

He didn't.

I slowly cocked the revolver. The sound was as loud as a double handclap in the now-silent store. Behind and all around me, I could hear customers and employees scrambling for cover.

"Drop it," I said again. "Last chance."

This time he dropped it, and the pistol too, and thrust both hands high in the air. Still pointing my gun at him, I took a step back, kicked the device out of the way, and asked a lady standing nearby to call the police. She just gawked at me, but the woman beside her took out a cell phone and started punching numbers. With my free hand I ripped open the front of the big guy's shirt, but all I found there was a giant white belly. Our potential thief was also a liar.

I didn't wait for the cops to arrive. I handed my revolver, which was of course still empty and still had the price tag attached, to Eddie—he had picked up the "bomber's" dropped pistol and was standing there holding the duffel bag—and left. Once again, I could feel the amazed eyes of a group of people, watching me leave. On my way out, I heaved another sigh. I had planned for that gun I'd been studying to be hidden in my pocket right now, along with a box of fifty .38 cartridges I had also planned to steal and take home. So much for that. My plan for petty larceny had been petty as well.

I could hear the beginnings of cheers and applause coming from all the way back in the sporting-goods section as I stepped out into the street. I saw that the skies had cleared now, the earlier storm only a dark gray stain on the eastern horizon.

I didn't mind walking—I'd done a lot of it, lately—but all of a sudden, I felt tired. At least it wasn't raining.

What a go-round this had turned out to be.

Almost an hour later, when I returned to my neighborhood, I saw several dozen people gathered in front of my house. Most were folks I recognized but didn't really know, and several of them detached themselves from the crowd and walked out to meet me. One was a short man in his forties—a Mr. Walters, I thought—walking alongside the old lady who'd kicked my wannabe mugger and questioned his ancestry, and two others were the parents of the deaf boy. The boy stood between them. Everyone was grinning like they'd won the Powerball lottery.

Mr. Walters said, "My ma told me what you did for her today, and I told these people. The cops picked up the guy you knocked out—"

"That bastard," his mother said.

"—and everybody already knows what you did for this boy here."

The deaf kid's parents had tears in their eyes, and when they heard this, both of them came forward and squeezed me so tight, I saw stars. The mother was openly weeping now, and within ten seconds my right shoulder was soaking wet.

"Also," Walters continued, after I'd disengaged, "a policeman came by looking for you a few minutes ago and told us what happened at the shopping center earlier. Said the store wants to give you some kind of award, and if you still haven't found work, they'd like to hire you." He grinned even wider and patted my dry left shoulder. "We're proud to know you, Mr. Longwood. All of us. We're proud to have you as a neighbor."

By the time the last of the crowd dispersed I'd shaken so many hands my fingers were sore, and when I got upstairs my phone was ringing off the hook. I let it go. I had too much to think about, right now.

Slowly I took my almost-empty wallet from my pocket, opened it, and removed the suicide note I'd written last night, the one telling Annabelle how her love was a thorn without a rose, always causing pain but never providing beauty—and that I'd finally decided to blow out the flame. I re-read it, gazed out the window at the neighborhood for a long time, then refolded the note and tucked it back into my wallet. I figured I could always try again tomorrow.

Or maybe not.

I Don't Want to Miss a Thing
(From the Armageddon Soundtrack)
Leone Ciporin

The prospect of going to Callie's wedding terrified Bridget. They were family, and she had to attend, but it was all she could do not to grab the wheel from Troy and turn the car around.

"Who are these friends of yours we're meeting, Brid?" Troy asked lightly.

"High school buddies." While Callie, Jake, and their wedding party gathered at the rehearsal dinner, the high school crowd had organized their own gathering, a preview of their approaching five-year reunion.

Callie and Brid were kissing cousins, almost literally, because they'd both kissed Lucas behind the bleachers. But when it came to prom time, one cousin was enough, and he'd chosen Brid.

"What's that grin for?" Troy asked, as he turned onto a country road. Maple trees dappled his face, shading one sunglassed eye.

"Just remembering old times." Sometimes Brid missed Lucas so much, her whole body ached. Troy was good at ferreting out information. She dreaded what he might find out.

"Remembering old boyfriends?" Had he read her mind?

Brid scooted as close as her seat belt would allow. "That was before I met you."

His hand grabbed hers. "I know you wouldn't cheat on me, babe." He squeezed her hand so tightly, her finger bones crunched together.

"You're the only man for me." She loved Troy so much. How could he not know that? His devotion thrilled her; he'd never abandon her like her father had done. Her father had kissed the top of Callie's head one morning, and moved out while she was at school.

And then there was Lucas. She still couldn't believe he'd chosen to abandon her.

They passed an overgrown field. Brid pointed to scraggly flowers clinging to the side of the road. "Dandelions. Like on our first date." She met Troy on a cold February day during their college sophomore year. She'd been huddled on a bench in the quad, recovering from a good cry, when Troy approached, dandelion in hand, telling her she was too beautiful to be unhappy.

Now, as she stroked Troy's cheek, he leaned into her touch. "I can afford to give you nicer flowers these days, babe."

"You take good care of me." Brid rubbed a spot behind his ear.

They pulled into the restaurant parking lot, and Brid slipped on her small leather backpack, a clone of the one her father had given her for her tenth birthday. For her eleventh birthday, he'd sent a card and a check.

Troy held the door for her, placing his other hand on the small of her back to guide her in. Brid loved how Troy touched her. Her father used to ruffle her hair or squeeze her shoulder.

As they entered the room reserved for dinner, Brid stepped closer to Troy, hoping everyone would see how much she was loved. Unfortunately, the first person she saw was Selena, the classmate she most feared Troy meeting. She and Selena had never gotten along, even in high school. Though Brid had gained a few pounds since then, Selena still had the curvy figure that had given her such power over boys. Even the quarterback followed her down the hall as she tossed him flirtatious glances.

Selena aimed one of those glances at Troy. "Look at what you brought in, Brid. You must've hired a high-class escort service." She laid a hand on Troy's arm and purred, "Because you seem too good for her, sweetie."

Brid smiled as Troy arched an eyebrow. Selena had miscalculated; Troy didn't like pushy women. Brid circled a hand around Troy's other arm. "Still in the market, I see, Selena. Perhaps someday you'll find a boyfriend too." She rested her cheek on Troy's shoulder.

The edges of Selena's mouth curled up. "Oh, I'm married. My husband's at a business dinner." Her glare turned icy. "And, while you always could find a man, Brid, you couldn't always keep him."

Lucas. Brid's stomach turned icy.

Selena tipped her head at Troy. "Nice to meet you… Brid didn't tell me your name?"

"It's Troy." His expression mixed curiosity with confusion, both of which worried Brid.

Brid pointed at a cluster of people near the buffet table. "Let's go meet my friends."

Selena gave a finger wave as Brid led Troy away.

"What was that comment about?" Troy whispered in her ear.

She had to tell him. He'd find out soon enough. "My high school boyfriend, Lucas, killed himself in college. Jumped off the library tower." She waved at a couple inspecting the buffet. "Please, I don't want to talk about that. Let's say hi to these folks." She wiped an emerging tear.

After a brief mingle, everyone filled their plates and took their seats. Brid chose a table with people she hadn't known well in school. Lucas's name didn't come up again and she relaxed.

But, on the way to the hotel, Troy said, "Tell me more about Lucas. Were you two serious?"

Brid's stomach went cold again. "He died three years ago. Before I met you."

"We've been dating almost three years, so it couldn't have been too long before that." His forehead furrowed. "You never mentioned him. Anytime I ask you about yourself, you keep saying there's nothing to tell. And now I find out about this past love?"

Brid scrambled for an answer. "That day we met when I was sitting on the bench, trying not to cry? I'd just visited his grave. That's why I was so upset."

Troy was silent for a moment, then said, "Did you know he was suicidal?" At the violent shake of her head, he said, "Were there problems in your relationship? Was that why he did it?"

"No, not at all." Brid searched for the right words. "We only grew apart after we went to different colleges. No big fight or anything, it's just that the long-distance thing didn't work." That was what Lucas had called it, "the long-distance thing."

Troy said, "If you and I were in different cities, would we stay together?"

"Why would we be in different cities?" Brid clenched her hands to stop them shaking. "If we moved away, we'd move together, wouldn't we? You wouldn't walk out on me?"

She couldn't bear being abandoned again. She still cherished that glorious Sunday with her father, reliving it in her mind. He'd taken her to a movie, a romantic comedy she still watched once a month, and then to lunch at her favorite pizza place. On the way home, they'd stopped for ice cream, laughing together as chocolate ice cream dribbled down her waffle cone.

The next day, he moved out. She'd only seen him a handful of times since.

"Of course, we'd go together." Troy gave her an incredulous look. "I wouldn't leave without you."

Brid felt a rush of love for him.

That night, Troy gave her a dandelion he plucked from the sidewalk and cradled her head as she had a good cry over Lucas. All the old memories had flooded back, and she felt as if he'd died only yesterday. Troy didn't ask questions. He simply held her and ran his fingers through her hair. She closed her eyes, feeling his gaze on her as she drifted into sleep.

Brid put on extra foundation the next morning. If she could just get through the day without Lucas's name coming up again, she'd be fine.

The wedding was at three o'clock, timed for a dinnertime reception. Callie's parents had money, and they'd gone all out. The church was massive, with vaulted ceilings and a wide aisle lined in blue and white ribbons. Despite its size, the space filled quickly, with ushers efficiently guiding guests to their seats, placing Brid and Troy on the bride's side.

The organist launched into the wedding march, prompting a parade of bridesmaids dressed in navy blue, tucking their hands around tuxedoed elbows, followed by the bride and her portly father, both his chins held high.

Callie's dress was spectacular, highlighting her narrow waist and well-endowed chest. Brid noted the beaded train, fluted sleeves, and intricate lace surrounding the scooped neckline, storing them in the wedding plans section of her mind.

Troy whispered in her ear. "She's showing a lot of cleavage for a bride."

"I'd never wear a wedding dress that low cut," she whispered back. She felt a thrill of pleasure at discussing wedding plans with Troy. His hand rested on her knee.

The minister intoned the vows. "For better or for worse, until death do us part." Brid put her hand on top of Troy's, to seal that future promise. Someday, they would be making those vows. She'd wear a dress he approved of.

After the service, a line of cars clogged the two-mile stretch between the church and the reception. As they stopped and started, Troy said, "Now that you're finally telling me a little about yourself, did you have a lot of boyfriends in high school?"

"Just Lucas." She touched his shoulder. "I've always been a one-man woman."

"Good." His voice was clipped. "Because I'm a one-woman guy. I've been cheated on before. I told you about that." He gave her a hooded glance. "I don't intend for that to ever happen again."

Troy had told her about Janine on their first date, how they'd met the first day of college, gotten serious fast, and talked about a future together. Until the night Janine told Troy she had to study late. He'd gone to dinner with friends and caught her cuddling another guy in a corner booth. He learned she'd been dating the guy for weeks behind his back.

"I would never do that to you." Brid fumbled for a tissue to blot the sweat seeping through her double-layered foundation.

"As hard as it was to talk about, I still told you all about Janine right up front," Troy said. "But I never heard a word about Lucas until now." His jaw stiffened, and his hand on her leg gripped so tightly her thigh ached.

Brid gritted her teeth at the pain in her leg. "That hurts, babe."

He took his hand away but didn't apologize. She knew who needed to apologize. "I should've told you about Lucas, talked more about myself. What can I do to make it up to you?"

"Let's discuss it later. We're here." He slid his Dodge Ram into a parking spot and escorted her inside, his hand guiding her by the elbow as she cradled their wedding gift. She'd picked it straight from the registry, the nicest item she could afford: a plate from their china set. White, with a thin gold band that made it worth ten times what a plain white plate would cost.

The burst of flowers at the entrance probably cost thousands of dollars. Every stem was capped by a flower at the cusp of full bloom, all in shades of blue. At her own wedding, she'd go with dusky rose, though she could never afford this many flowers. After her father walked out, Brid and her mother had to leave their rambling Victorian home with the wrap-around porch and move into a skinny townhouse her mother struggled to afford, even with child support.

Inside the reception hall, tables with spindly chairs encircled a parquet dance floor anchored by a decorated table for two, waiting for the newlyweds. In the meantime, guests plucked hors d'oeuvres and made the most of the open bar.

A curly-haired boy hovered by the wedding cake, his father snatching him back mid-reach. Brid smiled at the boy as he trotted past. Their children would inherit Troy's wavy blond hair and green eyes, but hopefully, they'd have her small, straight nose, her favorite feature. They'd grow tall too. Brid was tall, and Troy stood a full head above her.

Selena's nasally voice pierced Brid's fantasies. "I see you brought Mr. High Class again."

Brid's irritation turned to terror when she saw the man standing next to Selena.

Selena smiled. "You remember Billy Reilly? We're married now."

Senior year in high school, when Lucas seemed to be losing interest, Brid flirted with Billy, even went to a football game with him, to make Lucas jealous. It had worked.

Selena purred. "Troy, I'm sure you know the history—"

Brid cut Selena off. "Of course, I remember you, Billy. We sat next to each other at the homecoming game."

As Troy and Billy shook hands, Troy said, "Nice to meet you, Billy. Let's go get the girls' drinks." Brid's fear dissipated as the two men took a step toward the bar.

But Selena would not be stopped. She raised her voice so the men could hear. "Troy, did you know Brid once dated Billy? Made a big play for him." She pointed at her husband. "He ended up with the right woman, though."

"Congratulations on your marriage." Brid hoped she sounded casual, but Troy threw her a quizzical look before following Billy to the bar. She debated following him, to explain.

That could wait. "Nice to see you, Selena." Brid had never uttered a bigger lie. "But I have to find our seats." She spun around and walked away, forcing herself not to run.

Selena had never forgiven her. She'd get back at her by making Troy think Brid was a cheater. Those tall blond children with straight noses would never be born.

Brid found their table, settled into her seat, and took deep breaths to calm herself. She needed a clear head to get through this.

As soon as Troy arrived at the table with their drinks, she pulled him to her. "Selena is trying to make you mad at me because I sat next to Billy at one game, and she got jealous."

Troy pushed his gin and tonic to one side. "You didn't cheat on

Lucas with Billy?"

Sweat beaded behind her ears. "Not at all. Selena was always afraid of that—she was crazy about Billy—but all I did was sit next to him at one game."

"Not just any game. You said it was homecoming. Did Lucas know you were with Billy then? Where was he?"

"Of course, Lucas knew." She'd made sure of that. "He had a family funeral that weekend."

"What about the homecoming dance? Who'd you go with?" He pressed his hand against her thigh, still sore from his earlier grip. "I can't believe you've never told me these things."

Brid mentally blocked the ache in her leg. "I didn't go to the homecoming dance at all. Lucas was away." She'd hated staying home, but now that lonely night was a good thing. "Like I said, I'm a one-man woman."

Troy's chair clattered to the ground as he stood. He righted the chair, and growled, "I'm going to walk around a bit."

He strode away, straight toward Billy. Brid held her napkin to her lips to block the drop of bile that rose from her throat. What if Billy told him he'd taken her to the game? That it had been a date?

Fortunately, the band began playing, signaling the wedding party's arrival, and sending everyone scurrying to their tables. Brid gulped Cabernet to wash away the sour taste in her mouth as Troy returned to his seat.

Their table appeared to be the "remote relatives" table, rather than the "high school friends" table. Brid made small talk with Callie's other cousin and introduced herself to Jake's chatty aunts. She resented not being included at the "high school friends" table until she realized Selena and Billy were there; she silently thanked Callie.

Servers delivered a dinner of Cornish game hen, butternut squash, and brown rice. Despite her upset stomach, the food tasted good. The hen was moist, rosemary-flavored. They'd gone top dollar.

The thought of planning her own wedding calmed Brid through the first few toasts. She beamed as Jake ended the toast to his bride with a lingering kiss. The maid of honor's tribute was touching, and the best man's toast made Brid chuckle.

But her stomach roiled again as Selena rose to her feet and raised a glass. "I'm so glad to be here today, celebrating my friend's wedding." She waved her glass toward the couple. "And she's marrying a wonderful guy." Her voice wobbled. "But there's one person I so wish could be here to see it." Selena glared at Brid. "Most of us still can't believe he left us." She sat abruptly.

At Troy's questioning look, Brid whispered, "She's never accepted Lucas's suicide."

Troy gripped his knife and stared at her. "Sounds like she blames you."

"I'd just told him I thought we should see other people, because of the long-distance thing." Brid laid a hand on his arm.

Troy dug his knife deep into the game hen, pulling a piece from the breast and shoving it into his mouth as he watched Brid.

She signaled a server to get Troy another drink. Troy was a sleepy drunk, not an angry one, and more alcohol would ensure a peaceful night.

Troy was halfway through his second gin and tonic when Callie's father led her to the dance floor for the father-daughter dance. He looked so much like his brother, Brid's father. Brid's throat is clogged. Her father hadn't even come to his niece's wedding, choosing his wife's family reunion instead. Would he show up at her own wedding? Would he walk her down the aisle? With a new wife and a new daughter, he had no time for her.

Brid's breathing steadied again by the time Callie and Jake paraded onto the parquet floor for their first dance, swaying to the Ed Sheeran song Brid was considering for her wedding song.

Other couples joined the bride and groom. As she and Troy danced, Brid peeked over his shoulder at Callie and Jake, fingers intertwined as they greeted guests. At the edge of the dance floor, Jake's aunt and uncle hissed at each other over who had cheated on their diet more. The curly-haired boy marched past, his mouth lipsticked with wedding cake icing.

That night, Brid sat up in bed, watching Troy's deep, drunken slumber. His eyelids flickered and his hand twitched. She hoped he was dreaming of her. She could stay awake all night, watching him sleep.

During her last visit to Lucas's college, they'd gone up to the library's rooftop patio late one night. Lucas said he wanted a private talk, and she hoped for a ring. When he said they should see other people, she shoved him. She only wanted to stop him from breaking up with her. But at least Lucas died as her boyfriend, not her ex. He died still belonging to her.

She told police Lucas was upset after she broke up with him. They questioned her several times, and people were wary for a while, but in the end, the story stuck. Except for Selena. She knew Brid would never break up with Lucas. Yet, without evidence, her claims had simply sounded like a natural disbelief that Lucas was suicidal.

Brid wiped a sliver of drool from Troy's cheek. He would belong to her forever.

Drop Dead Gorgeous

(From the album, Just Push Play)

M.E. Proctor

"He'll want her done with, Harry. His kind ruminates on vengeance like a heifer chews the cud."

Harry McLean wedged his back in the corner of the velvet-upholstered booth and stretched his long legs on the seat. Now, without having to turn his head, he had a good view of the bar and the knock-out blonde perched on the central stool.

"He wants his money back, Luis. He doesn't want her dead."

"Keep telling yourself that, maybe you'll sleep better at night." Luis Garcia took a sip of his Canadian and Seven. "Mama didn't carry me in her belly all the way from San Salvador to see me working for Ray Castellan."

"You're not working for Castellan, you're working for Diana."

Somewhat true. When Diana Galindo told Harry *DG Investigative* had been hired by Castellan to find the woman who had conned him out of three million dollars, Harry's first reaction had been: *Good for her!* Anybody smart enough to hit the cartel lawyer in the wallet, where it hurt the most, deserved his heartfelt admiration. Then, what Diana said sank in.

"He *hired* us?"

In his previous life as a cop, Harry had spent countless hours trying to nail Castellan. The thought that part of his salary would come courtesy of the slime lawyer was enough to sour his whisky without adding lemon juice.

"Would you rather he ask his south-of-the-border buddies to track her?"

"Once we find her, he'll call them anyway," Harry said. "We'll just make it easy for them to chop her head off. Drop the case, Di. Let the woman run and take her chances."

They argued. Harry threatened to quit. Diana compromised.

"We find her, we get Castellan's money back, and we set her on her merry way. Is that acceptable, Harry? You realize recovering the money makes the case a lot more complicated."

The case was complicated from the start. It might have been the toughest Harry ever worked on, and that was without even considering retrieving the money. The woman had a talent for changing names and appearance. She also found gullible marks with baffling ease. Some of them went to the cops to lodge a complaint—which is how Harry caught the trail—but most stewed in anger and silent humiliation. And she raked in the dough. She could have hopped on a plane and enjoyed her hard-earned wealth in the sun, but she was greedy. Castellan's millions got company.

Harry set eyes on her for the first time two months earlier in a posh suburb of Chicago. Her hair was short and brown then. He thought he had time to build a trap, but she skipped town before he could spring it. Then he missed her by a hair, a bright red hair, in Atlanta. Here, in Miami, she went by Charlotte Wainwright, was ash blond, and affected a British accent. She wore the name, the hair, and the plum grammar well. Vowing he wouldn't be caught flatfooted again, Harry asked Luis Garcia, the agency's Miami associate, to lend a hand. At this point, another line item on the bill wasn't likely to make Castellan squeal. He'd been paying through the nose for months.

Luis waved at the server and ordered refills. "How do you want to play it? We let her work the con and catch her when she collects? It looks like she's got a bite."

Charlotte had been getting more bites than she could handle from the moment she hoisted her perfect butt on that stool. Marks had been circling, mouth open and teeth bared. No surprise. She was an appetizing long-legged morsel in a cocktail dress that didn't come from the outlet mall. With what she netted she could afford haute couture. The men thought they were sharks when they were chum. They came in all sizes and were mostly middle-aged. The club had fake retro Rat Pack vibes, done in chrome and glass with a generous helping of sleaze and hard liquor. Charlotte rose above it all like a pagan idol in a corny B-movie. The set was cardboard, but the technicolor was luscious. It matched her heartbreak of a smile, Marilyn before the fall. Harry felt pangs of impurity. He feared he was falling in love. Or lust, rather.

"Let's see what dude she picks." Harry wished he was wearing his nice suit. Draped in it, he would run rings around these doofuses. The Hawaiian shirt and khakis dumped him in the tourist drawer. He should have planned better. Luis could step in, however. His good looks and dark blue silk suit were yacht club ready. Or wiseguy. Or narco in a *Miami Vice* episode. Harry hadn't put the suggestion to Luis yet. He didn't have to.

Luis smiled. "If you want me to put my natural modesty on the line, just say the word."

That was the biggest bonus of working with true professionals. They didn't need a road map or an instruction manual.

"It looks like she's zeroing in on the baldy with the red tie," Harry said.

"Flat ass and a beer gut. Does she go horizontal with them?" Luis lit a cigar in cocky disregard of the rules. Nobody objected because nobody cared.

"She's pitching hedge funds and real estate deals for serious money. When she opens her legs, she loses credibility."

They nursed their drinks and watched the show at the bar. Charlotte hit the perfect temperature. It was miraculous how she skated between high-society Ice Queen and Hot Cookie. Real talent. The more Harry watched her perform, the more impressed he was. If he hadn't known she was baiting a line, he would never have guessed it. What did she tell these guys, that she was waiting for her date and he was late? She'd been there since eleven. It was inching toward midnight. Something would happen soon.

"He'll take her back to the hotel," Harry said. "If I'm right, he won't stay long."

Harry had a hotel room on the same floor as Charlotte. For five days, Luis and he had been watching her door. Stakeouts were boring, by definition. At least, they weren't in a car. They had access to coffee and a bathroom.

"How long does it take her to work a mark?" Luis said.

"A couple of days. She's efficient."

Charlotte never stuck around after a con. She hit fast and ran even faster. Harry knew he missed an opportunity tonight. He should have worn the suit and made a move. His desire to pitch his brains against hers, and challenge her at her own game, was so acute it hurt.

The bald guy with the red tie's entire body leaned toward Charlotte. She might be talking financials, but the dude had something else on his mind. She flashed him a bright smile and slid off the stool. Heads turned to watch her walk to the restroom. There was no swaying of hips. Harry thought she must have practiced that straight walk before a three-sided mirror.

"Maybe they give her the money in the hope of getting laid," Luis said.

"Obviously it works." Harry slipped out of the booth. "I'll settle our tab. It's wrap-up time. Better if you leave first."

Luis was out of the club before Charlotte emerged from the restroom. Harry was hunched over the bar counter, signing his credit card slip. She came so close to him that he could smell her perfume. Something expensive, enticing. A hint of cherry. Is that what she tasted like? He lingered, got another whiff of her scent, and shuffled to the exit, with regret. He was halfway there when a man walked in. A thought flashed through Harry's mind: *That's him. Charlotte's date. The guy who made her wait.* It was complete nonsense. Charlotte didn't have a date. It was the excuse Harry imagined she gave for being at the club. And yet. The man was perfect. Tall, dark, criminally handsome, brushing forty, in a pale linen suit wrinkled just right, a glint of gold on the wrist. As if he'd been cast and costumed for the role. Harry had stopped in his tracks and forced himself to move. He glanced at the scene one more time as he opened the door. The man was at the bar. Charlotte had swiveled on her stool. She faced the newcomer. The guy in the red tie was forgotten.

* * *

Harry called Luis as soon as he set foot on the sidewalk. "Change of plans. It looks like she's going to dump the mark."

"For the fashion plate with the Porsche?" Luis chuckled. "Hey, it can't always be work. Girl's allowed to have fun."

Harry bit back an acid retort. Charlotte awoke his worst possessive tendencies. He had been hunting her for too long. There always came a moment in a protracted chase when he started to believe the prey belonged to him.

"He drives a Porsche?" Harry didn't see the car in the parking lot.

"Gave the keys to the valet who didn't waste a second taking it for a spin," Luis said. "I called the plate in. It could be a rental. Guy splurging on cool wheels for a weekend, getting his investment back in chicks."

Harry groaned. He wasn't in the mood for waiting another hour in his car, just to watch Charlotte wrap herself around that hunk. "Can you handle it? Stay on her. I don't give a shit about the man."

"*Sin problema.*"

A long shower, maybe a little nap to look forward to. Harry swore he would wear the suit next time. No more portly pigeons. He could act the part and handle Charlotte. If he had moved in tonight, he would have bagged her before the sexiest man alive swaggered in. Diana didn't like it when he injected himself in a case, but they had wasted too much time already. Their client was bound to lose patience and call in the muscle.

Harry hummed under the hot shower. *I'll seduce her to save her life.* Damn, she was a gorgeous piece of woman. And damn, he couldn't get her out of his head.

He was checking email—Diana wanted a status report, she was getting impatient too—when his phone rang.

"He's parking the car in the hotel garage," Luis said. "Looks like he plans to stay the night."

Harry spat out a curse. He opened the laptop camera app showing images from the hallway, deserted this time of night. He saw the couple leave the elevator. The man had an arm around Charlotte's waist. She leaned against him. Very romantic. She swiped her room card, and he pushed her through the door. His hands went up her skirt.

Harry leaned back in his chair. His fingers trembled on the keyboard, and he made a fist to stop the shaking. He was angry. And furious at being angry. The click of the door opening brought him to his senses.

"The Porsche is not a rental," Luis said. "It's leased to a business in Coral Gables. Diamond dealers. Looks like our girl has lucked out again, even if she has to put some skin in the game this time."

"I need a drink."

Luis poured two stiff whiskeys. The bottle was half full. Booze made watchers sleepy. They tried to stay away from it. "She's a thief, Harry. You know how the story ends. She'll be arrested and locked up. Or she'll trick a nasty chump and get hurt. Or despite what you're trying to do, Castellan won't forgive and will send in the cutthroats. She's the wrong crush, buddy."

"Yeah. Sure." He took a long swallow, and let out a snicker. "I'm glad we didn't bug the room."

"Now you're putting ideas in my head," Luis said. "You mind taking the first watch?"

Harry straightened in the desk chair. "I'm too hyped to sleep anyway." And he wanted to see the Porsche playboy leave. The faster he got out of there, the better.

No such luck. When Luis took over at three in the morning, the man was still in the hotel room.

* * *

"Harry, wake up."

Luis was grabbing his shoulder.

"She's leaving."

"What?" Harry was at the computer in two steps. He saw Charlotte, dressed in jeans and a sweatshirt, standing by the elevator at the end of the corridor. She carried a leather bag. Her purse was slung over a shoulder. The time was five-thirty. "The Porsche guy?"

"No sign of him. He must still be asleep."

Maybe. Maybe. "You go after her." Harry felt a shiver between his shoulder blades. "Keep your distance. Traffic is minimal. She'll spot you in no time. She's good, Luis, very good."

"We have the tracker on her car anyway."

"Yeah, and if she takes the Porsche, we're screwed."

Luis was out of the door at a run. That left Harry pondering. The sensible thing to do was go to reception, show his detective license, and get somebody to open the hotel room. All that took time he didn't have. He rummaged through his travel bag and exhumed his lock pick set. He slipped on a pair of gloves.

A blast of cold air hit him in the face when he opened the door of Charlotte's room. The air conditioning was cranked to the max and fighting the morning dampness that came from the open terrace doors. It didn't completely mask the smell.

The man was on the bed, face down, naked. The ivory handle of a knife stuck out the side of his neck. He must not have struggled much because the bed sheets were still tucked in. They were soaked red. A fresh kill.

Harry went around the bed, careful to step over the dead man's clothing and shoes. A gun lay on the floor, dropped on the man's jacket, on the right side, near the night table. Harry peeked in the bathroom. The shower looked pristine. It was an illusion. Charlotte must have been covered in blood. Luminol would paint the stall blue. She had removed all her personal items, and the closets were bare. It was doubtful she had managed to wipe off all the fingerprints she'd left during her extended stay. And the DNA. On the dead guy. There was no doubt who he was. Ray Castellan had lost patience indeed. He had sent a hitman.

Harry went back to his room to pack and called Luis.

"She took the Ford," Luis said. "I have it on screen. She's heading north."

"Fuck caution. Get closer. She's going to ditch the car. How far is she from the airport?"

"Fifteen minutes at most. You want me to stop her? She's sticking to main roads, Harry. I can't shove her off the shoulder."

A beat. What was the plan? "If she's going to the airport, you'll have to intercept her in the parking garage or the terminal. Grab a tracker when you leave the car so I can find you."

Luis was a pro, but Charlotte had an edge. An airport was a good place to get lost, and she wasn't running blind. She had stayed in that hotel room with a corpse long enough to clean up, pack, and check early flights out of Miami. There wasn't anywhere she needed to be, meaning she could go anywhere, and then anywhere again from there. All before a maid found the body and the cops started scrambling.

Luis did well. He caught up with Charlotte in the parking garage and followed her to the North Terminal. She stood in line at check-in and dropped her bag. Luis caught her before she went through Security. He was charming and a fast talker, and it served him well. Charlotte didn't make a scene. She didn't want police attention any more than he did. He handed her his phone.

"Harry wants to talk to you."

"Who the hell is Harry?"

"An admirer."

Harry was running through the parking garage, a few minutes away. "I've tried to have a conversation with you since Chicago."

"What for?"

"I don't want you to miss your flight, Ms. Wainwright, or whatever name you're using now."

That silenced her.

"There must be a coffee shop nearby," he said. "I'll meet you there."

* * *

Her make-up was much lighter than the night before and there was a slight shadow under her eyes that had not been there. Stabbing a man and watching him bleed to death could do that to a girl. She was still drop-dead gorgeous.

Harry smiled. "You made me run, Charlotte."

"I didn't ask you to, Harry. Who are you working for?"

"A detective agency. Ray Castellan hired us."

She paled under her light tan.

"You need to get him off your back, Charlotte. You can't deal with him and the cops at the same time. You can't keep the money."

She pouted. "He tried to kill me. That's worth something."

Harry laughed. "You want a discount? What about your life as the gift in the kiddie meal?"

She leaned on the small bistro table, closing the distance between them. There was that whiff of perfume again. "What guarantee do I have?"

"None. But if he has you killed *after* you make restitution, the entire world will know he's a vengeful piece of shit. You will hold the moral high ground."

She burst out laughing. "Six feet under. How come you didn't try to entrap me?" She pointed at Luis who stood discreetly to the side. "Or him. He's cute."

"We missed our chance last night." Harry handed her a piece of paper. "An account number and a phone number. If you call the number, you'll get confirmation that the account belongs to Castellan. I won't stop you from getting on that plane, Charlotte. What you do when you get to your destination is your choice."

She pocketed the note. "You trust me to return the money?"

"There's always another con." Harry stood up. "Choose your targets more wisely. You know the saying. When it's too good to be true…"

She shouldered her bag, gave him an ironic little nod, and left the café.

Harry watched her go through the security screening. She was wearing flats, not the high heels of the night before, and she wasn't keeping her hip swivel in check like she did at the club. Harry had a feeling she knew exactly the effect she had on him. After all, he'd been watching her for a long time. Why would he stop watching her now?

Jesus is on the Main Line
(From the album, Honkin' on Bobo)
Tom Milani

Gail stood next to Mary, watching David place the packages into the suitcase. They were the size of bricks and wrapped in clear plastic. He handed Mary a sheet of notebook paper with a hand-drawn map. A sketch of a church was at the end. "Just put the suitcase under the altar," he said, as he continued to work. "Nothing to it."

A rogue wave of nausea hit Gail, and she ran into the bathroom. Mary held her hair back as she threw up. Afterward, she rinsed her mouth in the sink, avoiding her reflection in the mirror. When they emerged from the bathroom, the suitcase was zipped closed.

"You need to pull yourself together," David said.

"I'm fine," Gail said. The nausea had passed, and whatever moral or ethical concerns she had about the contents of the package were outweighed by a single practical consideration: she and Mary needed the money.

David walked them to the box truck, already loaded with expensive outdoor furniture they were delivering to some rich bitch who lived on the Eastern Shore and never tipped. He wedged a screwdriver into a slight gap in the floor to raise a hidden panel and put the suitcase inside.

* * *

Abner faced his congregation. They peered up at him, swaying like the shadows cast by the candles running the length of the church. Lately, he'd been possessed by a vision of his church burning, the fire engulfing the parishioners, their cries rising, along with smoke and ash.

To forestall that vision, he looked at the church ceiling, an inverted vee of exposed wooden beams supporting ranks of planking. The candlelight didn't reach the peak, so what he perceived was an emptiness, like the void in Genesis before God created light.

He bowed his head toward his congregation. "Let us pray," he said.

* * *

"Pull over," Mary said.

"Here?" Gail asked.

"See the church?"

Gail eased the box truck onto the shoulder. The air was still and heavy, the day's heat soon to come. They got out of the truck, and Mary began wading through a stand of thigh-high scrub, her hair haloed by the late morning sun. When they first met, Gail had initially dismissed Mary as blissfully ignorant, one of those girls who moved through life untouched by tragedy or heartache. Still, she'd never known anyone less guarded, and at a time when Gail felt everyone around her had ulterior motives for whatever they said or did, that was welcome.

She joined Mary on a narrow band of ground marbled with clay. Beyond them stood the remains of a church. Windowless and roofless, the building was a ruin. Garlands of ivy climbed the outer walls, the earth reclaiming them. A plaque said the church had burned down in 1940 and that Abner Prentice, the pastor, had died rescuing two boys from the fire.

"Are you sure this is the place?" Gail asked.

"Don't you feel it?" Mary said. She spread her arms as if taking in a breeze. If anything, Gail thought, the air had grown even more still, more silent. She just wanted to get through this day.

"Gail—" Mary started.

She fell in slow motion—knees buckling, arms collapsing, head lolling—before Gail caught her. Mary's eyes rolled so that only the whites showed, her body rigid, her jaw trembling.

* * *

In his sermon, Abner told his flock that Jesus was always listening to their prayers, and that it pleased Him to know what they wanted. After the service ended and the parishioners had gone, he crossed the path to his living quarters. More cabin than house, the building contained a small bedroom and kitchen. The living area was crudely divided by a room he'd built himself to serve as his office. There he wrote his sermons and counseled members of his congregation, providing comfort to those who'd lost their faith and mediating disputes among others with more earthly concerns. Abner still believed in the message of the Gospels, but he'd begun questioning why God had chosen to fill his head with visions. Overlaid on the reality before him like an animator's cell, they caused him to lose focus and stumble.

He changed into canvas work pants and a flannel shirt and carried his ax to the woodpile. Some of the parishioners would frown at his labor on the Sabbath, but Abner reasoned if he could preach and lead them in prayer, which was its own kind of work, then surely this labor would be permitted.

The aged wood split easily, and the rhythm of setting each log on the stump, swinging the ax, and stacking the quartered logs cleared his mind. Soon, he was barely aware of the sounds the ax made as it split the wood. Even his own exertions—his steady breaths, the rustle of his clothes—failed to register. His movements mechanical and fluid as an automaton's, he lost all sense of himself and his surroundings.

Two young women approached him, one holding the other as in the *Pietà*. Abner stopped mid-swing. He found himself drawn toward the woman being carried, the pull so strong he dropped the ax and took a few steps forward, before falling to his knees.

* * *

Mary's body went soft as if deflating. Her eyes fluttered open. Gail cradled her head in her lap and patted her cheeks.

"How long was I out?" Mary asked, her voice a whisper.

"Just a few minutes," Gail said. "Longer than last time," she couldn't help adding.

Mary didn't seem to hear. Gail helped her sit up. The neurologists they'd seen gave Mary a tentative diagnosis of epilepsy, but lacking insurance, they couldn't afford the imagery the doctors ordered. The medication they prescribed was expensive and left Mary so disoriented Gail felt as if she were living with a stranger.

So, they were delivering drugs for David.

He was an old college boyfriend who took their breakup hard, but they'd stayed in touch. The deal he offered them wasn't without risk, but short of a miracle, Gail couldn't get Mary the care she needed.

Now, she thought their adventure was over before it had really started. "We have to turn back," she said. "This can't be the right place, and you need to see a doctor."

Mary ignored her and picked her way across the charred timbers that had spilled from the church until she stood in the entrance. The doors were long gone, but the mortices for the hinges still held bits of rusted metal. Beyond the entrance, a single shaft of light pierced the interior at an angle. Dust motes within it twirled like something alive.

Gail turned on her phone's flashlight and panned the space. "It's not safe to go inside," she said. The light only reached a few feet into the church, but it was enough to reveal that the floor was gone. The joists that remained were warped, some dangling like girders over blackened earth.

Mary stepped forward as if the floor were intact, and soon Gail lost sight of her. Gail's heart pulsed like a fist to her chest. She couldn't bring herself to follow Mary.

Voices came from within. Mary's—and a man's. A wave of cold passed through Gail, and she shouted Mary's name. Her words seemed trapped within the church.

* * *

Now the woman who'd been carried stood in an angled shaft of light, her features shimmering, indistinct. Her thick hair framed eyes that radiated warmth and kindness. Abner couldn't look away.

She motioned for him to stand. Facing her, he couldn't gauge the distance between them, yet he felt the measure of her love. It was a force, like gravity or magnetism, the physics beyond his understanding.

In the distance, the other woman came into focus. From her he sensed fear, not of him, but of whatever afflicted the woman she'd carried.

Abner closed his eyes. "Jesus, make her well," he said, less a prayer than a request. When he opened his eyes, the shaft of light was dimming, the woman within becoming less substantial by the second.

"Don't go," he pleaded.

"Save the boys," she said.

Abner found himself alone in the yard, facing his church. The windows glowed red, the paint on the mullions blistering. He wrapped a handkerchief around his hand and yanked open the door. The sound of the fire was somehow worse than the flames. It crackled and roared as if its power came from something animal. Paint sloughed from the plaster-like dead skin, and gray smoke billowed against the ceiling.

A whimpering from beneath the altar drove him forward. There he found two young boys cowering, one of them still holding a box of blue-tip matches. He bent and scooped each boy under his arms. "Close your eyes," he yelled. A wall collapsed behind him, forcing him toward the nave, which burned like a pyre. He ran through a gap in the flames. The boys screamed as he stumbled outside, finally releasing them. They scrambled away, staring at him with fear in their eyes. Abner wanted to tell them that God forgave them, but before he could get the words out, smoke seized his throat, and he collapsed.

⋆ ⋆ ⋆

"Who were you talking to?" Gail asked. "I heard a man's voice."

"It was the pastor," Mary said. "He wanted Jesus to help me." She faced the church ruins. "I saw the fire. He saved two boys."

Gail shivered. The voices had been real—she knew what she'd heard—but the fire had happened long ago. What Mary claimed to have seen must have been suggested by the plaque.

Gail spread the map across the hood and ran her finger along the route David had drawn. "We pulled over too early," she said.

"This is where we are supposed to be," Mary said. "Can't you feel it?"

What Gail felt was an animating presence in Mary, a newfound focus and strength. Still, she worried it was temporary. "We need to get going, or we'll be late." They'd left early in case of traffic delays, but that margin was gone now.

They got in the cab, and Gail drove south. A half-hour later, she saw the cop car in her side-view mirror, a flicker of blue and red lights as the cruiser crossed the center line, the driver's face hidden by windshield glare. She eased the truck onto the shoulder, and the cop pulled in behind them.

Gail killed the engine and rolled down her window. Driver's license and truck registration in one hand, both hands in plain sight against the wheel, she stayed focused on the side-view mirror.

The cop who stepped from the cruiser sauntered—there was no other word to describe how he walked—toward her. His face bore none of the impassive lack of emotion she was accustomed to seeing from authority figures. Instead, he seemed amused, as if he were in on a joke she and Mary were to be the butt of. They hadn't been speeding, and Gail had gone over the truck before they started, checking for damaged reflectors, burned-out bulbs, and anything that would give a cop an excuse to pull them over.

"Ma'am, please step out of the vehicle," he said, not even making the pretense of asking for her license and registration.

Gail knew her rights, and she knew reality, so she did everything in slow motion, keeping both hands in sight. When the cop told her to leave the paperwork on the front seat, her heart sank.

He led her to the back of the truck and motioned to the roll-up door. "I need you to open that."

He wore shades, so she couldn't read his eyes. His tone was still amused, but she sensed an edge behind it. Another cop pulled up. Gail guessed this must be what passed for excitement around here. Since they'd left the church, she'd only seen a handful of cars.

The other cop joined them. Taller and leaner than the first, he wasn't even pretending to be friendly.

"The other girl is in the cab," her cop said.

Tall and Lean stalked the length of the truck and returned with Mary, his hand encircling her bicep.

"She's not going to overpower you, cowboy," Gail said. "Lighten up on the grip." Her cop grinned, but Tall and Lean shoved Mary onto the hood of the first cop's car and snapped handcuffs on her wrists.

Gail started toward Mary. "She didn't do anything."

Her cop blocked her way, holding up a finger. "Take one more step, and you'll be bent over the hood next to your girlfriend."

Gail's fear and sense of helplessness roiled her insides, and she stepped back. Her parents' warnings to her as a teenager hadn't prepared her for this.

Her cop's posture eased. "That's better," he said. "Now, why don't you tell me what's inside the truck."

"Patio furniture," she said.

He laughed, doubling over. Gail saw Tall and Lean jerk Mary upright. She shook herself from his grip, and he looked at his hand as if he couldn't believe she'd so easily broken loose.

"Jesus, make them set us free," Mary called.

Her cop shuddered before straightening. "It's going to take more than Jesus to help you now," he said.

Gail heard the doubt in his voice, even though she knew that the cops must have gotten to David, and he'd given them up. The idea that he would get caught before them never occurred to her.

Her cop nodded at the roll-up door. Resigned to the scene that was going to play out, she unlatched it, then hoisted herself onto the bumper. She grabbed the handle and raised the door.

"I'll be damned," her cop said.

* * *

Abner's congregation formed a bucket brigade. Flames and smoke gave way to the hiss of steam. It emerged like fog from the spaces where the doors and windows had been. The church's roof was gone, and tongues of char lapped the walls.

The fog rolled toward Abner until the space around him was infinite and empty. His church was destroyed, but the boys were safe. A furrow formed in the fog. Abner traced it with his eyes. At the other end stood the woman he'd begged not to leave. This time she was alone.

"You came back," he said.

He sensed that she was stronger now. Whatever afflictions she'd faced were gone. The space between them was clear, not shimmering as before.

"To thank you for your prayers," she said. "And to tell you that your work is done."

Below him, his congregation shed no tears. Instead, Abner listened as they began making plans to build a new church. When he looked up, the woman was gone, a white light glowing where she'd stood.

A star without heat, his salvation made manifest, Abner headed toward it.

* * *

Tall and Lean pushed Mary against the side of the truck and removed her handcuffs. Her cop told them to unload all the furniture, and they spread the chaises and glass-topped tables and chairs across the swale beyond the shoulder. It was an unlikely site for a garden party, Gail thought, and wondered if the heat had addled her mind.

While they worked, cars slowed. Gail saw a few cell phones peeking out and knew videos of their arrest would be online soon.

After they finished, her cop jumped onto the bumper. "Oh where oh where could it be?" He pretended to look around the back of the truck before squatting beside the panel in the floor, just a foot from the opening.

Making them remove the furniture had been a charade. To add some legitimacy to the search, Gail supposed. Or because it amused her cop. He unfolded a knife and slipped the blade under the panel. She and Mary stood at the shoulder's edge. Her cop lifted the panel and set it aside. From the cavity in the floor he removed a zippered suitcase, smiling at Gail like Christmas morning. He hopped from the truck, and Tall and Lean joined him.

Her cop pulled the suitcase to the edge of the bumper. "There's some serious weight here," he said. "What do you think?"

Tall and Lean hefted the suitcase. "Enough to put these bitches away for a long time."

"We're not bitches," Gail said. "Show some respect." If she was going to jail, she'd do so with her head held high.

Both cops glared at her until her cop started laughing. Tall and Lean joined him, but his laughter sputtered like a weapon. "Before we bring you in, I'll teach you about respect."

Gail refused to look away.

"Enough with the preliminaries, am I right?" her cop said to Tall and Lean. He finally turned when her cop unzipped the suitcase and raised the lid.

"What the hell?"

He pulled out a box of gauze, then a package of Ace bandages, then tubes of antiseptic before finally upending the suitcase. Bottles of isopropyl alcohol and hydrogen peroxide spilled onto the bed of the truck.

"We have a delivery to make," Gail said. "May we go?"

Tall and Lean and her cop turned toward them. "No, you may not go," her cop said, all humor gone now.

"Give me your knife," Tall and Lean said to her cop.

He jogged down the swale and began slicing the cushions on the furniture. "Hey," Gail yelled. "We have to deliver that."

Her cop grabbed her from behind and slammed her onto the hood of his car, the impact knocking the wind from her. Her arm bent into the small of her back, he kicked her legs apart and pressed against her, his face inches from hers.

"I will not be played by you. Now you tell me where those drugs are, or I will conduct a body cavity search on you and your friend in front of everyone."

Gail bit down on her anger and fear until it came to her what to say. "It's David, isn't it?" she started. "He's still angry I left him for Mary."

Her cop's weight lifted. "Did you find anything?" he called to Tall and Lean. He didn't reply.

Cars were honking now as they passed. A news helicopter hovered above them. Gail waved, and a cameraman gave her a thumbs up. In the distance, more police headed their way.

A woman in a pantsuit got out of an unmarked car. She took Tall and Lean and her cop aside. Gail couldn't make out the words, but she was doing all the talking, and they were looking at their feet. When she was done, her cop and Tall and Lean began loading the furniture back into the truck.

"You're free to go once they're finished," the woman said.

"What about all the damage they did?" Gail asked. "Who's going to pay for that?"

The woman glared at her cop and Tall and Lean before facing Gail again. "Tell the owner to call me." She handed Gail a business card. "That's my direct number."

Gail wondered if the videos had already gone viral or if the woman they were delivering the furniture to was politically connected. Probably both, she decided.

Once they were on the road again, Gail tried to work out what had just happened. She turned to Mary. "David wanted to get back at me for breaking up with him, but he didn't want to lose the drugs. So he switched out the suitcases when we were in the bathroom. I don't know what he planned to tell the cops, but—"

"Don't complicate things," Mary said.

Gail decided that if Mary needed to believe it was divine intervention that got the cops to let them go, she wasn't going to press her on it.

Mary took her hand.

Some kind of energy passed between them, Gail comprehending the simple truth in what Mary had said. They were free, and Mary was well. Gail believed. She stepped on the gas, the road ahead clear.

Street Jesus

(From the album, Music from Another Dimension!)

Jim Winter

Sgt. Jeff Kagan rarely kicked in the door to an interrogation room. He did so this time. At least, it was heartfelt.

The redheaded frat boy smirked at him. "My lawyer will get me off."

"Did you hear the words, 'You are under arrest' followed by 'You have the right to remain silent…'?" said Kagan. "No? Guess what. You call a lawyer at this point, I start calling you a suspect."

The boy scoffed. "My dad will—"

"Your daddy will lose a lot of city contracts." He slapped an iPad on the table, making it sound like it hit harder than it did. "I'm assisting Homicide on this case. If Captain Ryland kicks it over to Special Investigations, I'm putting my top detective on it. She eats punks like you for breakfast and doesn't shit out the bones when she's done."

He tapped the iPad, bringing up a picture of a man nailed to a cross. Dressed in a loincloth and obviously dead, bloody spikes protruded from his wrists and his feet, though one of the feet had slipped. "Coroner says he was alive when someone did this to him." He leaned forward, scowling. "And you and your buddies pointed and laughed. So, you think it's funny someone got crucified in 2023 Ohio?"

"Yeah," said the kid. "Some homeless darkie gets nailed to a cross the day after Good Friday—"

Kagan slammed his fist on the table, making the iPad jump. "Mr. Bailey, I'm about five seconds from slapping an obstruction charge on you. This is Monticello, not New York. We don't have night courts, and the courts here don't open until Tuesday after Easter weekend. Anyway, does your buddy Caine know you like the word 'darkie'?"

"Token's different," said Bailey. "He's from Holland Island."

"No, but you call him 'Token.'"

"Don't you watch *South Park*?"

"I'm more a *Family Guy* fan." Kagan leaned back in his chair. "You're a person of interest, Bailey. You could be a suspect. You could be a witness. You could just be an asshole making my job harder than it needs to be. So, you and your little buddies are going to sit in your own personal interrogation rooms until Detective Griffin completes her leg work."

"She has nice legs," said Bailey, his eyes lighting up as if the comment might save him.

"And now a me-too moment at the expense of a woman who currently owns your balls." Kagan rose. "I'm a dedicated cop, Mr. Bailey, helping Detective Griffin because I used to work for this squad, and this case is so fucked, it might end up in my squad. I'm clean, but my dad was the dirtiest cop who ever served on the force. The one thing I learned from him?" He leaned in, making sure the SIG Sauer on his hip showed under his jacket. "I am absolutely fucking ruthless."

Bailey tried to give him the thousand-yard stare. It faded as Kagan stared back.

* * *

In Homicide's bullpen, Kagan took the usual shit from his former coworkers. The sergeant of Siberia, they called him. Never mind Special Investigations had become the mayor's pet project. For years, it had been a dumping ground. And some of the dumpees remained, though they could consider their exile well behind them.

He took a seat opposite Lexy Griffin, still relatively new to Homicide. She had established herself quickly, however. Slender, usually dressed like a corporate attorney with coppery hair, she might have appealed to Kagan's Irish blood. But years on the force told him to never date a cop. Besides, his wife might not have appreciated it.

Today, Griffin had her hair clipped back, a Monticello State sweatshirt replacing her outlet-mall blouses. It made Kagan smirk as he somehow always managed to at least throw on an Oxford and a tie, another thing his father had beaten into him. "I didn't expect you back from the morgue so soon."

Griffin did not look up from her iPad. "Oh, this is a rush job. Man gets crucified in the alley next to Old St. George, and upstairs wants a lid on it before the news gets it." She held the iPad up. "The man's been known only as 'Street Jesus' for years, so I don't think his fate is ironic."

The picture showed a nominally black man on the slab at the morgue in Vodrey Heights. Nominally, since he was also paler than Kagan's younger brother, a dark Irish computer nerd who lived mostly in his basement with a bank of computers. The victim, however, simply had that pale skin tone.

"If he's Street Jesus," said Kagan, "you'd think he'd be a bit more sunbaked. What do we know?"

She took back the iPad. "I stuck around for the autopsy. He was crucified post-mortem."

"And here I told Bailey he was alive when it happened.

"Let him think that. We haven't found the victim's clothes other than the loincloth. Who wears a loincloth these days? I don't even think they wore that during the Norman Conquest."

Kagan sipped from a cup of McCafé French roast, a vast improvement over the Big Lots Coffee the old Homicide captain provided when he worked this squad. "I'm not much on history. I know about the Troubles, and how my grandpa got out of Ulster five minutes ahead of the Prods putting one in his skull. Deservedly, according to my mother. Does the campus Lord and Savior have a name? Besides Jesus?"

She tapped at the iPad and brought up a dossier already put together on the victim. "Fortunately, the forensics tech thought ahead and sent in the prints. Our would-be messiah was one Isaac Watson, late of Beaumont Heights in Rock Ridge. Charged a few years ago with his wife's murder, but the Rock Ridge Division found the real killer. Burglar who'd already killed three other residents in various neighborhoods. Watson had a drinking problem and still believed he killed his wife." She pulled up Watson's autopsy photo again. "Here's the weird part."

As she blew up the picture, the dead man's right hand came into focus. In the palm were scars from two rather large puncture marks.

"These are on both hands," said Griffin. "And there are a couple in each foot as well, but the spikes used last night made them hard to spot."

Kagan's cup stopped halfway to his mouth and sank as his hand slowly moved back to the desk. "Are you saying this man was crucified before?"

"Strange, I know. But we're Irish. We believe mothers and hangovers are heavy penance. Some will have themselves nailed to a cross as an act of contrition. Mind you, they tie them up with ropes and use the nails to simulate a real crucifixion. Most people survive it."

"But not our boy Isaac."

"Like I said, dead before they hung him up."

"Want me to go round up witnesses?" asked Kagan.

Griffin smiled. "The sergeant asking the mere detective for permission? I'm honored. And no, I'll do it. You go ahead and grill the Four Horsemen of the Fratpocalypse."

* * *

Ken Morgan, the "cute one" if one wanted to compare them to the Beatles, had jet-black hair and a thin mustache. He could probably be a male model. Instead, he hung around with three other degenerates. He also darted his eyes from side to side, a rat looking for an out.

Kagan strolled in with his iPad and sat down. He said nothing, merely stared at the boy.

"My dad will have his lawyer here—"

"When we give you a phone call," said Kagan. "We only do that for suspects. Are you a suspect, Mr. Morgan?"

"Why am I here?"

Kagan repeated his person-of-interest spiel, much more calmly this time than with Bailey. "So, do you need a lawyer? Because I haven't used the words, 'You're under arrest.'"

Morgan stared at Kagan and blinked.

"That's what I thought," said Kagan. "Now, what were you four doing at the end of the alley? And why was it so funny to see a homeless guy killed on a cross?"

Again, Morgan stared, blinking.

Kagan's father would have slapped him to get him to talk. Kagan promised himself he would be a clean cop. Mostly. The filth was still hard to avoid even these days. "I asked you a question. Two, actually." When Morgan still said nothing, Kagan snapped his fingers in the boy's face. "Come on, pretty boy. Time's a-wastin'."

As though waking from a dream, Morgan shook his head, squeezed his eyes shut, and seemed to focus now. For a moment, it seemed he'd ask where he was and how he got there. "Right. Street Jesus."

"Street Jesus. What do you know?"

Morgan chuckled. "Just a freak who's wandered around campus since I started at State. Wears that stupid white robe of his. Says he was 'crucified for our sins.'"

"According to the coroner, he was. Twice. Though nothing like what was done to him last night. Do you know anyone who would want to kill him?"

"Ba—" Whatever Morgan wanted to say, he bit down on. "Bastards go around harassing the homeless. You know how someone sets them on fire?"

"Abandoned river docks in Prussian Meadow." Kagan smiled. "You seem to know a lot about that, Kenny. Since they die in the wrong part of town, it doesn't make the news. At least, not until sweeps month when Channel Four orders the I-Team to sensationalize something that'll let them gouge Toyota for more ad money."

"If you live on campus, you know."

Kagan nodded slowly. "And my associate, Detective Griffin? She's on said campus right now. Is that going to bear up? Or are you pissing on my leg and telling me it's raining?"

Morgan's brain appeared to lock up again. That tended to happen when Chads like him realized they were neither invincible nor untouchable.

Before he could find his voice to call for a lawyer, Kagan stood. "Tell you what, Kenny. I'll go talk to your buddies while you work on your story. 'Kay? That Randy Bailey guy looks like a real charmer."

As he exited, he noted to himself how his father would have put a fist through Bailey's teeth and told his rich daddy how unfortunate it was his son's face planted onto a table corner. Fortunately, Kagan was not his father.

* * *

Griffin dropped her purse on her desk as Kagan walked back into Homicide's bullpen.

"Rough day?" he asked.

"I stopped at the bakery on the other side of the alley from the church." She dropped into her seat, almost bouncing it. "Do you know what the shop owner calls our deceased?"

Kagan took his seat, holding yet another mug of coffee. "Got me."

"'Negro Jesus.'"

The mug stopped halfway to Kagan's mouth. "What?"

"Show me he dresses in a hood and white robe without him wearing a hood and white robe."

Finally, Kagan took a sip. "Did he tell you anything useful?"

Griffin blew out her breath. "He said he chased him out of the shop often, but some of his employees, mostly college students, gave him free bagels and water. Said he couldn't trust a man who crucified himself and didn't drink coffee."

Staring at his own mug, he said, "I'm with him on the second part. Sounds a little obsessed. Where was he last night?"

"Man's not Catholic, so not at Old St. George. Sent a Harbourtown squad to his house to confirm he was at home last night. We'll probably get a complaint."

Which, in Kagan's experience, would get shut down with, "It's a homicide investigation, sir. Someone was killed." If need be, someone could point out they hadn't hauled the man in as a suspect. "Let him whine. Anything else?"

"One of the employees knew him," said Griffin. "A Stacey Mobarry. She works at the shop. Said our vic walked around campus, seldom bothered anyone. He mostly listened."

"Listened?"

"Yeah. He would sit on benches with people and listen to them unload. Another thing. He never called himself 'Jesus.' Everyone else did. Even the priest at Old St. George."

Kagan crossed himself, more out of old reflex than any real reverence. "Speaking of, do we have an alibi for him?"

"Mrs. Snyder," she said, "the live-in housekeeper for the rectory, says Father Gabriel was there all night."

"Are we sure she's not covering for her boss?" It wasn't unheard of.

Her right eyebrow went up. "How can Maria vouch for your whereabouts last night?"

"Oh." That story also wasn't unheard of. Priests couldn't marry. And not every priest wanted young boys. Not that Kagan saw a priest more than twice a year anymore.

Griffin sighed. "I guess it's down to Wayne, Garth, Beavis, and Butthead."

Wayne and Garth? Kagan hadn't heard that reference since he was a kid, back when Mike Meyers was still funny. "I got an idea." He pulled out his phone and hit a number on speed dial.

A breathless voice answered. "Kagan, someone had better have murdered the mayor for you to call me today."

"Ana," said Kagan. "Catch you at a bad time?"

"I'm hiking the slope in Big River Park," said Ana. "On my day off. Whattaya need?"

"Got roped into a homicide, a strange one. Lexy Griffin will send you the details."

"Wait. What? Kagan, I'm not even at home right now. And Melanie and I are—"

"Murdoch will take your Monday shift," said Kagan. "I need your magic fingers to look up anything you can on a guy named Isaac Watson, aka Street Jesus, over by Monticello State."

Ana's breathing slowed. She must have sat down. "Wait. Street Jesus is a suspect?"

"Victim."

"Shot?"

"Crucified." Kagan listened to a long, silent pause, slowly becoming aware of the traffic on the Inland Parkway below where Ana must have stopped on the trail. "Got your attention, didn't it?"

"What do you need?"

"Next of kin, anyone who might have a grudge. Just in case the four morons we have here at Settlers Commons turn out to be four potheads with rich daddies and nothing better to do the day before Easter."

"I'll be home in half an hour. Give me two hours after that." She hung up.

* * *

Kevin Donahue came from Kagan's least favorite background, pure Irish. Kagan's grandfather came from Belfast, which made Kagan a second-generation Ulsterman. It left him with a childhood where the "real" Irish, who still held a lot of sway in Monticello, lorded it over him. Now he had a badge on his belt. Donahue's reaction would tell him all he needed to know.

"So, coming in swing your dick already," said Donahue, his accent flatter than the steelworkers' kids Kagan had grown up with.

Kagan smiled. It gave him great pleasure to see some of the fire go out of Donahue's eyes. "You're a witness. If you don't want to become a suspect—"

"My father will—"

"Not appreciate his brat on Fox 18 while one of the bevy of blondes reports how you and your buddies stood and laughed at a man crucified on Good Friday."

"It wasn't on Good Friday."

Kagan's smile widened. "How do you know that?"

"I mean… Um… It was Saturday morning when you rounded us up." He stood.

"Sit down," said Kagan, who then barked, "Now."

Donahue sat.

Kagan dropped into his seat and leaned back. "Let me guess. You were next going to tell me how you and your pals aren't gangbangers, that we shouldn't be rousting you like common street thugs."

Donahue rolled his eyes. "My dad is a major donor to the Republican Party."

Kagan snorted. "In a Democratically controlled town." He wanted to slam the iPad down for effect but decided the tablet had taken too much abuse. "What do you know about that man?"

Donahue folded his arms and looked away.

"Do you want to go home? Or to Norwalk?" Musgrave County, of which Monticello was a part, built its largest holding facility in the suburb of Norwalk. "Because we've got some boys down there who just missed a felony conviction. I'm sure they'll think you got a purdy mouth on you."

Donahue squirmed now. "I meant you brought us in this morning."

"But I asked you about last night," said Kagan. "And you said this morning. Now. What. Do. You. Know?"

"Ask Bailey," said Donahue. "I want my lawyer."

"Why do you need a lawyer, Kevin?"

"I… I'm a suspect, aren't I?"

"I never said you were under arrest. However, you are a witness. And while Mr. Bailey and Mr. Morgan have been somewhat cooperative, you go right for an obstruction charge."

"My dad will make that disappear." His voice wavered. He managed to sit up straight.

"Really? Isn't that what the Treasury Department said to dear ol' Dad to get him to roll on the speaker of the house down in Columbus?

Are you sure you want to play this game?" He sat up. "What if I told you Bailey and Morgan sold you out, said you did it."

"Oh, come on! It took more than one person…"

Kagan rose. "I'll be right back. Maybe your friend Token has something to say."

* * *

The token was the black one. Why he tolerated the nickname escaped Kagan, as did why he would hang out with the three racist pricks in the other interrogation rooms.

His real name was Darius Cain. Of course, his name was Darius. Every black family on Holland Island with two C notes to rub together named their firstborn son after Darius Reed, aka Monticello's Joe Kennedy. Like Kennedy, Reed made millions in bootlegging during Prohibition. Like Kennedy with parts of Boston, Reed's family pretty much owned Holland Island, even the white neighborhoods. Cain's smirk matched Randy Bailey's when he walked in the door.

Kagan decided to catch him off-guard. "Before we get started, tell me. Why do they call you 'Token'?"

Cain looked at him the way Kagan looked at the average drunk during his patrol days. "Don't you watch *South Park*?"

"I'm more of a *Beavis and Butthead* kinda guy." He managed a Butthead laugh to punctuate.

Cain shook his head. "Gen X old fart."

"Okay, this is the part where you tell me your daddy is a fat cat lawyer and threaten me," said Kagan. "And then I tell you that you're a person of interest and don't have to give you a phone call until I talk to you. So, how about we skip the bullshit and get right to it? Why did you think Street Jesus on a cross was funny?"

Confusion clouded the younger man's face, but he followed it up with a scowl. "Come on, man. The dude goes around campus acting like Jesus. Even got nail marks in his hands, and you wonder why we were laughing? That was funny as shit."

"Well, your funny shit got him killed. And your buddies are ratting you out."

"Fucking Randy. Don't you have any other suspects?"

"Your three buddies. Detective Griffin is out interviewing witnesses. And I ruined another detective's day off to get info on any other suspects we might find. For all I know, Isaac Watson owed the Estradas money for his latest fix. Assuming he still used before his untimely death."

"Who's Isaac Watson?"

"Street Jesus." Kagan took off his jacket, letting Cain see the shoulder rig and the city-issued Sig Saur P320 in its holster. "Victim had a name, Cain. Granted, your dinner with momma tomorrow will cost more than Street Jesus probably panhandled in a week, but still, he had a name."

"You have a name," said Cain. "And that's intimidation."

"What's intimidation?"

"You parading around with a gun like that."

"I'm a cop. I carry a gun." He spread his arms wide. "And it's hot in here. Now, the sooner we get to the bottom of this, the sooner I can go home and watch the Guardians and the 'Stros. And the sooner you can go back to the Island and pretend to be a good Baptist boy for your momma."

"You're Irish. Aren't you supposed to be off this weekend?"

Kagan leaned onto the table, hands splayed out as he loomed in Cain's face. "I had tacos from the Phoenix for lunch yesterday. Last night, I had a bacon cheeseburger for dinner. Then I banged my wife half the night. I'll brag to my cousin, the priest, and call it a confession." He stood. "That give you some perspective? Now, who nailed Street Jesus to the cross? And did you kill him to do it? Or was it an accident?"

Cain folded his arms. "Lawyer."

Kagan knew it would come to that. But the boy's scowl told him all he needed to know. "It was Bailey, wasn't it?"

"Lawyer."

"Bailey thought it was funny to nail Street Jesus to a cross. What happened? Hit by a drunk? Where's your car, Darius?"

"*Lawyer!*"

"Whose car did you all take to the bars last night? Come on. I can't believe you four degenerates walked from Tau Sigma Phi all the way down to Old St. George."

"Lawy—"

"What am I gonna find if Randy Bailey's car is in the impound lot? Which it most certainly is by now."

"Ask Kevin," said Cain. "He'll back me up. Bailey hit him."

"And the cross?"

Cain seemed to deflate. "All Ken and Randy." He chewed his bottom lip for a moment. "Kevin and I watched. If you lean on Ken, he'll buckle."

Kagan smiled a satisfied smile. "My wife's an assistant prosecutor. I'll see what she wants to do with you. You can call your lawyer now."

He stepped outside and found Griffin getting ready to leave.

"Your pal Ana found a brother-in-law with a grudge," she said. "He never believed the burglary angle on Watson's wife. Swears Watson killed her himself."

"Cain just gave up Bailey."

One of her eyebrows rose. "Oh?"

"I'm going to call another detective on our squad, who's going to call one of her friends at Fox 18. Before these schmucks' daddies can squash the story, I want it smeared all over the city."

"You know the Chief's not going to like that." Griffin smiled thinly. "I used to date Carl Gammons at Channel Four."

"Harder to squelch the story with more than one station involved. Wanna go ruin Bailey's weekend?"

About the Contributors

Bill Baber's writing has appeared at crime sites across the web and in print anthologies—most notably from Shotgun Honey, Gutter Books, Dead Guns Press, Down and Out Books, and Authors on the Air Press—and has earned Derringer Award and Best of the Net nominations. A book of his poetry, *Where the Wind Comes to Play*, was published in 2011. He lives with his wife and a spoiled dog in Palm Desert, California.

John C. Bruening has been a professional writer since the 1980s, first as an award-winning journalist and later as a magazine editor and marketing specialist. He is the author of the Midnight Guardian series published by Flinch Books, a small press he co-founded in 2015 (www.flinchbooks.com). His short stories and essays have appeared in anthologies published by Flinch Books, Moonstone Books, Blue Planet Press, Becky Books, Stormgate Press, and others. He lives in a suburb of Cleveland, Ohio.

Leone Ciporin's short stories have appeared in *Black Cat Mystery Magazine*, *Mystery Weekly*, *The Saturday Evening Post*, *Woman's World*, and numerous mystery anthologies. She's a member of Mystery Writers of America and currently serves as secretary of MWA's Mid-Atlantic chapter. Leone lives in Charlottesville, Virginia.

Mary Dutta (marydutta.com) is the winner of the New England Crime Bake Al Blanchard Award for her short story "The Wonderworker," which appears in *Masthead: Best New England Crime Stories*. Her work can also be found in numerous anthologies, including the Anthony-nominated *Land of 10,000 Thrills: Bouchercon Anthology 2022*. She is a member of Sisters in Crime and the Short Mystery Fiction Society. Enjoy her blog at Writers Who Kill.

Eve Fisher's stories have appeared in *Alfred Hitchcock's Mystery Magazine, Black Cat Mystery Magazine, Mystery Weekly, Crimeucopia,* and elsewhere. She's been an Honorable Mention in *The Best American Mystery Stories* ("A Time to Mourn" in 2012 and "The Sweet Life" in 2022), and in *The Best American Mystery and Suspense* 2023 with "The Closing of the Lodge." All appeared in *Alfred Hitchcock's Mystery Magazine.* Her "Cool Papa Bell" appeared in Josh Pachter's *Paranoia Blues: Crime Fiction Inspired by the Works of Paul Simon.*

John M. Floyd is the author of more than a thousand short stories in publications such as *Alfred Hitchcock's Mystery Magazine, Ellery Queen's Mystery Magazine, Strand Magazine, The Saturday Evening Post, The Best American Mystery Stories,* and *The Best Mystery Stories of the Year.* A former Air Force captain and IBM systems engineer, John is an Edgar Award finalist, a Shamus Award winner, a five-time Derringer Award winner, and the 2018 recipient of the Short Mystery Fiction Society's lifetime achievement award.

Avram Lavinsky is a recovering musician with one gold record and countless unsold ones in his attic. He has been shortlisted for awards, including the Brooklyn Non-Fiction Prize, the Al Blanchard Award for New England's best crime story, and the Claymore Award for best YA novel in progress. His publishing credits include *Deadly Nightshade: Best New England Crime Stories 2022* and *The Best Mystery Stories of the Year 2023.* He's also earned starred reviews from the nation's toughest critics, his three teenage sons, although not often.

Steve Liskow (www.steveliskow.com) worked as a director, actor, producer, designer, and technician for 100 productions throughout central Connecticut before publishing his first stories. His wife played Lady Bracknell in one version of *Earnest.* Since then, he has published stories in *Alfred Hitchcock's Mystery Magazine, Black Cat Weekly, Tough,* and several anthologies. He has also been a finalist for the Edgar Award and the Shamus Award. His latest novel is *Words of Love.*

Jeffrey Marks is the Edgar, Agatha, Anthony, and Macavity nominated author who has written prolifically about mystery authors of the 1940s and 1950s, including *Who Was That Lady?* and *Atomic Renaissance.* He is currently working on a biography of Erle Stanley Gardner and a dual biography of the two men who wrote as Ellery Queen. In his "spare time" he is the publisher for Crippen & Landru, Publishers.

Tom Mead's debut novel, *Death and the Conjuror,* was an international bestseller, and named one of the best mysteries of the year by *The Guardian* and *Publishers Weekly.* Its sequel, *The Murder Wheel,* was described as "pure nostalgic pleasure" by the *Wall Street Journal* and "a delight" by the *Daily Mail.* It was also named one of the Best Traditional Mysteries of 2023 by *Crimereads.* His third novel, *Cabaret Macabre,* will be published in 2024.

Adam Meyer is a Derringer Award-winning and Shamus Award-nominated author whose short fiction has appeared in *Prohibition Peepers, Mickey Finn, Three Strikes, You're Dead,* and other anthologies. He is also the editor of *In Too Deep: Crime Stories Inspired by the Songs of Genesis* and the author of the novel *The Last Domino.* His screenwriting credits include TV series and movies for Lifetime, A&E, National Geographic, and others.

Tom Milani (tommilani.com) has short fiction published in *Groovy Gumshoes: Private Eyes in the Psychedelic Sixties, Black Cat Weekly,* and *Illicit Motions,* among other publications.

M.E. Proctor (www.shawmystery.com) was born in Brussels and lives in Texas. Her short story collection *Family and Other Ailments* is available in all the usual places. She's currently working on a contemporary PI series. The first book will come out from *Shotgun Honey* in 2024. Her short fiction has appeared in *Vautrin, Bristol Noir, Pulp Modern, Mystery Tribune, Reckon Review, Black Cat Weekly,* and *Thriller Magazine* among others. She's a Derringer nominee.

Ed Ridgley won a New Yorker Cartoon Caption Contest in 2010, the cartoon showing a bar scene with a bartender, a detective, and a ballerina. His caption (the bartender's words) said "The guy you're looking for waltzed out of here an hour ago." And he won *Alfred Hitchcock's Mystery Magazine's* Mysterious Photograph Contest, July/August 2023. Ed is writing a memoir about his 2018 hike to Everest Base Camp in Nepal.

Joseph S. Walker (https://jswalkerauthor.com/) has had short fiction published in *Alfred Hitchcock's Mystery Magazine*, *Ellery Queen's Mystery Magazine*, *Mystery Weekly*, *Tough*, and three consecutive editions of *The Best Mystery Stories of the Year*. He has been nominated for the Edgar Award and the Derringer Award and has won the Bill Crider Prize for Short Fiction. He also won the Al Blanchard Award in 2019 and 2021.

Jim Winter (jimwinterbooks.com) is the crime fiction name of science fiction author TS Hottle. As Jim, he is the creator of PI Nick Kepler and also *Road Rules*, an Elmore Leonard-type caper about a trip to Florida gone bad. His reviews have appeared in *January Magazine* and *Mystery Scene*. Additionally, he is an editor for Down & Out Books. His latest novel is *The Dogs of Beaumont Heights*.

About the Editor

Michael Bracken (www.CrimeFictionWriter.com) is the Edgar Award- and Shamus Award-nominated, Derringer-winning author of more than twelve hundred short stories, including crime fiction published in *Alfred Hitchcock's Mystery Magazine*, *Ellery Queen's Mystery Magazine*, *Mike Shayne Mystery Magazine*, *The Best American Mystery Stories*, *The Best Mystery Stories of the Year*, and many other publications. Additionally, Bracken is the editor of *Black Cat Mystery Magazine* and editor or co-editor of thirty-two published and forthcoming anthologies, including the Anthony Award-nominated *The Eyes of Texas: Private Eyes from the Panhandle to the Piney Woods*. In 2024, he was inducted into the Texas Institute of Letters for his contribution to Texas literature.